He wanted her to trust him, but how could she when everything he did just proved how untrustworthy he was?

Their eyes remained locked on each other, both searching for a sign that the other was going to be the first to end this standoff. A slight five o'clock shadow enhanced Luke's rugged good looks. Unfortunately for her, Jordan's stubborn streak was no match for her female hormones. *Of all the people I could have run into today, why did it have to be him?*

Her voice softened slightly. "I'm sorry for bumping into you." She saw the muscles in his face relax. She noticed his gaze was focused on her lips, no doubt recalling that same kiss she couldn't wipe from her thoughts. A hint of color appeared on her cheeks.

"I heard you'd submitted an entry and I was on my way over to wish you good luck. Is it the tall one in the crystal vase?"

She nodded in response.

"Your arrangement is spectacular."

"Thank you."

"You look beautiful, Jordan."

Luke's dimpled smile brought to life the

sensations she'd experienced every time she saw him. Suddenly, she felt lightheaded under his appraising stare, hating that he always had such an effect on her. Why did *this* particular man, the one she needed to avoid the most, always manage to make her feel like she was the only woman in the room? She swallowed hard to push down her emotions and repeated her earlier question. "What are you doing here?"

"I'm here with Anna."

The color drained from Jordan's face. "Anna! Anna's *here*?"

She's guarding a secret...one that, if it's discovered, will destroy everything she's worked so hard to gain.

In order to claim her inheritance, Jordan Shaw is forced to return to her hometown. She changes her name and opens a flower shop, praying no one will ever learn the truth about her past. But when she meets Luke Kincaid, her carefully-constructed walls come tumbling down...even though she's convinced he's married.

He's in love with two women at the same time...one of whom he's never even seen.

When Luke wanders into Jordan's flower shop to buy a gift for his mother's birthday, Jordan falls off a ladder and into his arms. But this encouraging beginning quickly turns to anger and accusations. What could he have possibly done to make Jordan hate him? And how can he have such strong feelings for her when he also finds himself falling for M.J.—a troubled young woman he has met only through her long-lost diary?

KUDOS for *The Journey to Jordan*

A contemporary romance...Add in a little suspense when her no-account father shows up to recover his stolen money from the old house where they used to live, and you have a lighthearted and interesting story that's fun to read. There's no sex, but I guess sometimes you just can have everything. The plot is strong and the characters well-developed. – *Taylor, reviewer*

I enjoyed the characters and found them, especially Luke, well-developed and complex. I didn't mind the lack of sex, since holding off until marriage to have sex seemed to fit Jordan's way of thinking, even though it is a little outmoded and old fashioned. There are some people who still think that way. Aren't there? There was lots of sexual tension, though, and that worked for me. I also thought the plot was strong, with some nice twists and turns. I wouldn't have minded seeing more of the bad guy, or even having Jordan in some serious danger, but that is just the kind of books I like. As it was, The Journey to Jordan was entertaining and enjoyable. – *Regan, reviewer*

THE JOURNEY TO JORDAN

Large Print

Debbie Lee

A Black Opal Books Publication

GENRE: CONTEMPORARY ROMANCE

This is a work of fiction. Names, places, characters and incidents are either the product of the author's imagination or are used fictitiously, and any resemblance to any actual persons, living or dead, businesses, organizations, events or locales is entirely coincidental. All trademarks, service marks, registered trademarks, and registered service marks are the property of their respective owners and are used herein for identification purposes only.

THE JOURNEY TO JORDAN ~ Large Print
Copyright © 2012 by Debbie Lee
Cover Design by Jackson Cover Designs
All cover art copyright © 2012
All Rights Reserved
Large Print ISBN: 978-1-626942-77-6

DEDICATION

*First and foremost, I thank God
for His love and guidance.
Without Him, this book wouldn't exist.*

*To Nicole and Katie, my beautiful daughters.
I love you more than words can express.*

*Thanks to all of my friends for their
support and encouragement.*

*A special thanks to the very talented
members of my writer's group:
Robin Christensen, John Coultas, Kevin
Draper, Ana Ferguson, and
Joanne Taylor Moore.*

*And last, but definitely not least, a special
heartfelt thanks to Lauri, Faith, Susan,
and Jack at Black Opal Books for your
overwhelming kindness and
extreme patience with me.*

Chapter 1

Sold it! What do you mean you *sold* it?" The young woman demanded, her voice filled with despair. She glared at the bank manager. "But Mr. Armbrewster, you knew I've been working as hard as I could to save the down payment. I only needed a few more months."

"I'm sorry, but we held it as long as we could. I'm sure you can find another place around here to purchase."

"My grandfather built that house. I was raised in it. How could you sell it without contacting me first?"

"The bank was under no obligation to notify you. We received an offer from someone else, and the deal closed about two weeks ago," the pudgy, balding man responded. He blinked at her from behind his large, oak desk and added, "That's business. Besides Miss, it's *just* a house."

"Not to me it isn't."

The shimmer of unshed tears in her eyes had no effect on the manager's heart of stone.

She couldn't believe she'd lost the chance to purchase her childhood home. Needing to see it one more time, she drove to the edge of town. Her stomach fluttered nervously as she turned onto the gravel road and eased her car down the long driveway. Tears rolled slowly over her bottom lashes as she stared at the house through her windshield. Memories...that's all she had left.

Luke Kincaid leaned his back against the rear quarter panel of the faded green pickup wondering if he'd made a huge mistake. With his legs crossed at the ankles, he slid his thumbs into the front pockets of his worn jeans. His well-trained eyes surveyed the weather-beaten exterior of the old house. The building sat back off the paved street down a long, gravel road, visible only to people traveling west out of town and then only for a short time.

It was a white, two-story Craftsman with a sweeping driveway that curved in front of the spacious porch. On the other side of the driveway, there was a section of ground edged with large stones, and in the center stood the remnants of a crumbling water fountain. His mind's eye imagined the lush, green grass that had once covered the area, but now there were only tangled patches of dead, overgrown weeds.

Luke had passed by this place hundreds of times and had always wondered about the story behind it. Who used to live here? Why didn't anybody seem to care about it anymore? Why had it been abandoned and left to deteriorate in the sun and the snow and the rain?

Peeling paint exposed small sections of bare wood peeking out here and there, and a few of the blue shingles were missing. Yet as his eyes scanned the outside of the house, all Luke thought was how grand it must have been in its day. And how he'd planned to remodel it into something new and fresh, while doing his best to keep the true character of the home intact. *I hope you know what you've gotten yourself into.* His inner voice of reason challenged the impulsive side of him, the one that had made the decision to buy this "fixer-upper."

Luke's plan was to renovate the old house

then sell it to somebody who wanted to open a bed and breakfast. They seemed to be popular nowadays in Oregon, at least that's what he'd heard at the last contractor's convention. No matter how successful his construction company was, it never hurt to have a little cushion, considering the ups and downs of the housing market. He had just signed the papers at the bank two weeks ago, buying the property for next to nothing. Luke hoped he could make a sizable profit, especially since he'd be doing most of the work himself.

This afternoon, he wanted to take some measurements and make a list of the supplies he'd need to get started. The rickety, wooden steps leading to the porch sagged and complained under his weight. "That's the first thing I need to take care of after it warms up a bit," he said aloud before drawing a quick sketch, noting the dimensions.

He turned the antique doorknob and, with a bump of his hip, entered the house. There was no need for a key; after all, there was nothing of value left to steal. The rusty hinges squeaked their protest at being asked to work after all this time.

Gutting the kitchen would be his first project inside the house. Luke measured the space for new cabinets and countertops then drafted a rough diagram of the layout on his clipboard, adding the specifications for new appliances. The next step would be deciding whether to put in ceramic tile or restore the wood floors in this room. As the late afternoon daylight started to fade, a chill filled the house. He knew he'd have to inspect the rest of the interior and the surrounding property another day.

Pulling the front door firmly shut, he walked to his truck and threw his notes onto the passenger seat before brushing the dust off his denim work shirt and jeans. He was anxious to get home so he could start working on his plans for the house. Patches of snow dotted the ground, but the driveway had absorbed the spring sunshine, and it was dry. Luke was thankful he wouldn't have to deal with mud getting tracked in during the renovation. With one last glance in the rearview mirror, a warmth spread through his heart and made him smile.

The outline of the house faded, barely visible now, obscured by the dust kicked up by the truck tires on the gravel road. Wondering about the consequences of his impulsive decision once again, Luke shook his head before pulling out onto the paved road and heading for town.

He was almost home when he remembered that tomorrow was his mom's birthday and he'd forgotten to order her flowers. Swear words shot from his mouth as he hit the steering wheel with the heel of his hand. Most of the time he ordered them online, but he'd been too busy with work and trying to get everything settled to buy the old house these last few weeks.

Glancing at his watch, he realized he'd have to hurry and find a flower shop before they closed. He was sure he'd seen a florist sign at the mall where he'd gotten his haircut last Wednesday. As a rule, he didn't pay much attention to places like that. It had been a long time since there had been a special woman in his life to buy flowers for, except his mother.

Driving around the crowded lot, he scanned the names of the businesses and, to his relief, there it was. The Petal Pusher. *Odd name,* he thought, but as long as they could deliver his order tomorrow, he didn't care what words were painted on the front window. He parked his truck in front of the quaint little shop. A bell chimed as he entered through the bright yellow door. Even though the store was small, the displays were colorful and creative, the owner had maximized the space without it looking overcrowded. Fragrances from all the different types of flowers filled the air. It smelled sweet and fresh, like a woman.

"I'll be right with you," a feminine voice called from out of sight on the other side of the shop.

"No problem," Luke responded. He went in search of the female employee, but paused for a moment to notice the different shades of roses in the glass display case.

When he rounded the corner he found a woman standing on her tiptoes at the top of a stepladder. She was reaching for a box high on a shelf. He noticed that her body was slender and fit, like an athlete's. Her hair was light brown, pulled back into a loose ponytail. She was wearing jeans and a pink T-shirt that hugged her feminine shape. Her small, round behind was about eye-level with him and he wondered if she would be embarrassed by his assessment. Luke liked what he saw.

"Do you need some help?" he offered.

"No, I've got it, thanks."

As soon as the words left her mouth, she

stretched a little too far to the right and lost her balance. Luke rushed forward, catching her in his arms. She let out a scream the same time the cardboard box and its contents of glass bowls crashed to the floor.

Suddenly, Luke was face to face with an attractive young woman cradled in his arms. She stared up at him wide-eyed, obviously shocked that she hadn't landed among the glass shards. As they gazed at each other, his heart began to pound. He'd never encountered eyes like hers before; they were a blue-green color, the same shade he'd seen in pictures of water off the Hawaiian coast. "Are you okay?"

Jordan Shaw couldn't speak. Heat raced through her veins. She was looking into the face of one of the most handsome men she'd seen in a long time. His arms were strong, but gentle, as he held her against his warm, masculine body.

Luke helped her stand and then steadied her while she regained her balance. Without warning, and for reasons he couldn't explain, he wished he didn't have to let go of this beautiful woman. A strong desire to pull her back into his arms washed over him.

Embarrassed by the fact that a customer

had saved her from falling to the floor, Jordan cleared her throat, self-consciously tucking a few wayward strands of hair behind one ear. "Um, yes. I'm fine. Thank you." Her mind reeled as she fought against the sensations her body experienced while being held in his muscular arms. The face of another handsome man from her past flashed through her mind along with the gut-wrenching memories he'd left behind.

"You can let go now," she instructed, re-adjusting the hard exterior she'd built around her heart to protect her from the pain good-looking men like him always seemed to bring with them. Those tingles and flutters were a trap to draw you in and make you vulnerable. Jordan refused to be sucked into that game again. She'd played before—and lost. Pulling her thoughts together, she straightened her clothes.

"Excuse me while I get a broom to clean up this mess." When she returned from the back room, she began sweeping up the glass fragments. As she reached for the dustpan she'd set on the counter, her fingers came into contact with the man's hand.

His gaze met hers, "Here let me help you with that."

His dark eyes flashed with electricity. Jordan felt it surge up her arm and come to rest in her heart.

She was just about to protest, but her voice was nowhere to be found. When the last pieces of glass were safely deposited in the trash, she brought out a hand-held vacuum to make sure all the tiny slivers were removed from the floor. Setting the appliance aside after making several swipes over the tile, she finally stepped behind the counter. "How may I help you?"

Luke wasn't sure what had just happened. One minute, the captivating eyes of this woman were soft as they stared into his, the next, they were cold and distant. But there was no denying that something powerful and real had passed between them in those few seconds—something he wasn't prepared for.

"I need to order some flowers to be delivered tomorrow. Sorry for the short notice." A sheepish grin lifted the corners of his lips. "But it's very important and I'll pay extra if I need to."

"It shouldn't be a problem, as long as I have the flowers in stock. Do you know what you would like or do you need to look through one of the sample books?"

Her voice's blunt tone was all business.

"I know what I want." He paused while Jordan took out an order form. "I'd like a dozen each red, pink, purple, and yellow roses. Could you please put them in a tall silver vase like the one in that picture over there?" He motioned to a poster on the wall by the display of artificial plants.

After Jordan noted his choice of container, he added, "Could you please add baby's breath and some greenery, too?"

"Of course, sir." She glanced up at him, wondering how a guy dressed in a dirty pair of jeans and work shirt could afford such an expensive arrangement. This wasn't a bouquet for a casual affair. The person he was sending these flowers to was obviously someone very special to him. "What's the address where you'd like these to be delivered?"

She repeated the address to make sure she'd written it correctly then raised her head again and looked at him. Jordan was met by a sexy smile, made even more devastating as deep dimples danced on each cheek. She tried to ignore the sudden and unwanted sparks surging through her.

"Do you have a card you'd like to send along with the flowers?" Her voice cracked slightly after the brief encounter with his charming brown eyes, dotted with flecks of gold. "If not, we have some small ones you can choose from." She pointed toward the end of the counter with her pen.

He reached over and selected a blank card with a feminine border. Taking just a moment to jot down a few words, he gave it to her.

Anna,
Happy Birthday Beautiful!
I love you!
Luke

After sneaking a quick glance at the card, she clipped it to the order form, totaling the cost for the flowers, including the delivery charge. "How would you like to pay for this today?"

She certainly didn't seem very friendly, Luke thought as he handed her a credit card. She ran it through the machine and, when the transaction was completed, she looked up at him. "Here's your card and a copy of the invoice, Mr. Kincaid. They will be delivered tomorrow before three o'clock."

"Please, call me Luke," he said.

A small, terra cotta flowerpot full of business cards sat next to the cash register...*THE PETAL PUSHER – Jordan Shaw, owner.* "It's been a pleasure, Jordan." Seeing the look of confusion on her face, he raised the embossed card wedged between his thumb and index finger, answering the mystery of how he knew her name. "Thank you for your help."

Just as his hand wrapped around the doorknob to leave, she stopped him. "Oh, Mr. Kincaid—"

He turned to face her. "It's Luke, remember?" he said with a wink.

Jordan stiffened. He'd just ordered an expensive bouquet of flowers for another woman, signing the card *I love you!* and now he was standing there flirting with *her*. What a jerk! Still, she should say something about what happened with the ladder. After all, she could have been seriously hurt. "I just wanted to thank you...you know, for earlier."

The way Luke's eyes danced when he looked at her caused sensations she'd buried long ago to rush through her again, and she didn't like it. Well...she *shouldn't* like it.

He could tell by the tone of her voice that she was still a little embarrassed. "You're very welcome, Jordan. It was my pleasure.

I'm always willing to help a beautiful damsel in distress," he said, adding a theatrical bow and a playful wave of his hand.

He headed home to work on his plans for renovating the old house. A new project always excited him, the step-by-step process of taking something worn and turning it into something new. Every now and then, he would find his mind wandering to the incident that afternoon with the pretty florist. He liked the way she'd felt in his arms and the look she'd given him. But then her demeanor had changed, confusing him. Not that he had the time, or the inclination, to concern himself with her, or any other female for that matter.

Shaking Jordan's face from his head, Luke once again turned his attention to the plans in front of him. But his efforts didn't last very long. Soon he caught himself smiling at the way her eyes had locked with his, and how for a split second he'd had the overwhelming desire to kiss her.

And that would've been a crazy thing to do, more than likely resulting in a swift slap across his face. Realizing he wasn't going to get any more work done tonight, he switched off the desk lamp and went to bed.

Even after Luke left her shop, Jordan felt confused by the unexpected feelings their brief encounter had stirred up in her. *Why do I always have to tangle with losers like that?* All the way home, his handsome face wouldn't fade from her thoughts.

Pulling into the garage, she could hear the familiar barking sound that welcomed her home every evening.

"Odie! Be quiet!" Jordan shouted as she walked into the house. "Yeah, I missed you, too."

Her voice was more gentle now as she reached down to ruffle his fur. The little tan and white terrier mix, who resembled Hollywood's Benji, was jumping up and down and running in circles. He was always so excited to see her at the end of the day. Laughing at his silly antics, she remembered the day she'd adopted him from the local humane society. He was quite a little character. He'd been the last puppy left from his litter and when Jordan walked by him, he tipped his head, emitting a low whine. Her heart had melted into a puddle on the concrete floor of the kennel. He'd been the "man" of the house ever since.

As Jordan fell asleep that night, Luke Kincaid's rugged face crept uninvited and unwelcomed into her dreams. She struggled to push aside the image of his sexy smile and masculine embrace, and kept reminding herself that she had no business thinking about him. He had a "someone special"—and that made him off limits.

Besides, Odie kept her from getting too lonely. He was her most loyal of confidants. The only male in her life she could trust without question.

Chapter 2

The next morning around eleven, Jordan was busy assembling the massive flower arrangement Luke had ordered when her assistant, Darcy, walked in. She only worked part-time running errands, sweeping, making deliveries and, on occasion, helping Jordan with the customers.

"Hey boss," she said, tossing her purse in the office. When she didn't get a response, Darcy looked at Jordan and could see that she was deep in thought. "G-o-o-d m-o-r-n-i-n-g." Her voice was louder this time, drawing out the words.

"Oh, hi," Jordan muttered.

"Where were you just now?"

Jordan wasn't in the habit of sharing her personal thoughts with Darcy, so she scrambled for an answer. "Just thinking about the annual flower show that's coming up."

"Don't sweat it, your designs are awesome. I just know you're going to win," Dar-

cy stated with youthful confidence and enthusiasm.

Smiling a thank you at her assistant, Jordan thought about how grateful she was for
Darcy's support. Jordan was a perfectionist
and would love for her creations to be noticed
by the state judging committee. Winning
would also give her the recognition she desired for all of her hard work, as well as being
good publicity for the business.

"That's a fancy combo you're working on.
Did the President come to town and nobody
told me?" Darcy asked with a chuckle.

Luke's handsome face flashed into Jordan's mind. She could feel her temperature
rise, remembering his dimpled cheeks and the
wink he'd given her. It caused flutters to stir
in her stomach again. She focused her attention back on the vase of roses, irritated by her
body's response to him. Especially since,
there in front of her, was Luke Kincaid's sincere and overwhelming declaration of love—
for another woman.

"This needs to be delivered before three
today. There are a few others ready to go, and
when you're done with them, you can come
back for this one."

"Okay, see you later."

After Darcy left, Jordan put the finishing touches on the extravagant arrangement and set it in the walk-in cooler to keep the roses fresh until this afternoon. As her thoughts wandered to what kind of woman warranted such an elaborate gift, Jordan also pictured the man who'd ordered it. Luke seemed like a normal kind of guy, but this bouquet said high-class and expressed deep affection. Forcing his face from her thoughts, she went into the office to work on some invoices that needed to be paid.

About one-thirty, the phone rang. "The Petal Pusher, may I help you?"

It was Darcy. "Jordan, I've got some bad news. After my last stop, I was heading back to the shop but the van got a flat tire. I called my uncle to come change it, but he can't leave work right now. I don't think I'll be back in time to make that three o'clock delivery. I'm really sorry," the young woman cried, rattling out her predicament in one flustered breath.

Releasing a heavy sigh, Jordan closed her eyes, rubbing her right temple, "Okay, just get back when you can."

"Sorry, I didn't know what else to do."

"I know. It's okay. I'll make the delivery.

Please tell your uncle that I said thanks for helping with the tire."

Jordan kept her tone calm, not wanting to make her employee feel any worse than she already did.

After all, it wasn't her fault.

"You bet. See you later." Darcy's voice was less anxious now, genuinely grateful her boss had been so understanding.

As Jordan hung up, Luke's face appeared once again. She had to admit that she *was* curious about the recipient of the flowers and was surprised at the sudden rush of nerves at the prospect of meeting this mystery woman.

Thankfully, she hadn't crushed all of the large boxes from her floral shipment yesterday, so she was able to use one of them to transport the massive arrangement. Hanging a sign on the front door to let customers know that she'd be back in a little while, Jordan locked up then loaded the flowers in her SUV.

Doing her best to avoid the potholes, she maneuvered her way through the residential streets until she found her destination. It was an upper class neighborhood with manicured lawns and long driveways. Jordan carried the bouquet up the steps and rang the doorbell.

When the door opened, there stood a stunningly beautiful woman.

She looked as if she'd just walked off a runway somewhere instead of sitting around the house in the middle of the afternoon. Her clothes and make-up were flawless. Rich auburn hair framed her face and lay in soft curls a few inches past her shoulders.

"I have a delivery for Anna Kincaid."

"Oh my! They're absolutely lovely!" Her voice was heavy with an exuberant southern accent. "He's such a thoughtful and precious man!"

After handing her the flowers, Jordan held out a small clipboard and pointed to the line on the delivery form marked with an X. "Could you sign here, please?"

"Of course, just let me set these down." The woman stepped out of view for a moment.

When she returned, Jordan noticed that there were tears in her large hazel eyes as she scribbled her name.

"Thank you so much."

"I hope you enjoy the flowers." Jordan smiled before turning to leave.

"He always remembers. Every year, no matter what. He remembers," the gorgeous woman whispered, her face beaming before closing the front door.

On the drive back to the shop, Jordan thought about the auburn-haired beauty and Luke. They made a perfect couple. She'd noticed a large, diamond wedding ring on the woman's left hand with what she guessed to be about a two-carat center stone. A twinge of envy rose up in Jordan. She had hoped that maybe...maybe what? That the woman would be ugly with a hump? That she'd refuse the delivery because she never wanted to see him again?

Well, neither of those had happened. The mystery woman was a vision right out of a glamour magazine with high cheekbones and a killer body. Add in her captivating southern charm, and you had yourself a definite ten on any man's testosterone scale. And she was Luke's wife.

The scrawled signature was difficult to read, but there was no question the first letter was an "A." The thought of how he'd acted yesterday in her shop, with his playful smiles and sexy wink, angered Jordan. He was married and she needed to remember that. He was nothing to her but a customer. She wasn't going to let herself get sucked into that kind of situation. Still, her pulse thumped a little faster at the memory of being held in his arms.

The best thing to do now was forget the whole thing. She'd never seen him around town before and she prayed she never would again.

When she arrived back at the flower shop, Darcy was there. "How'd that last delivery go?"

"Fine." The word came out harsher than Jordan intended.

"Are you mad about the tire?" Darcy asked tentatively.

Jordan was lost in thought and didn't really hear her question. "What?"

"I asked if you were upset with me about the tire. My uncle and I took it to the auto shop and got it repaired. I'm sorry I couldn't make it back in time for that big delivery."

"No, it wasn't your fault. Sorry if I snapped at you. It's been a long day, and I'm just tired, I guess," Jordan lied. "Please, thank your uncle again for me and if I owe him anything for fixing the tire, let me know."

"Okay, will do. Do you need me to do anything else for you this afternoon?"

Jordan took a moment to glance around the shop before she answered. "Could you please take out the trash before you go?"

"Sure thing." Darcy carried the black, plastic bags to the dumpster out back and re-placed the ones inside with new bags for the next day.

Jordan was in the front of the store taking inventory of the flowers and supplies she'd need to order the following week.

"Bye boss, see you tomorrow," Darcy hol-lered from the workroom on her way out.

Before Jordan could reply, she heard the sound of the back door shut.

❀ ❀ ❀

Luke had been busy over the last couple of weeks between running his construction company and renovating the old house when-ever he had a spare moment. So far, he'd gut-ted the kitchen and rebuilt the front steps. Benny and Carl, two guys from his construc-tion crew, helped him clear away some debris one afternoon. The new cabinets and counter-tops were going to be installed next week and Luke wanted the trash hauled off before then.

"What possessed you to buy this old place?" Carl asked. He and Luke's dad had been close friends. When Luke's dad died,

Luke took over the business. Carl was the crew foreman and Luke's right-hand man. "You sure took on a big project here."

"I think you're right." Luke chuckled as his eyes scanned the house. "It was just something I needed to do."

Benny came around the corner, brushing the dust off his shirtsleeves and pants, before joining the other two men standing in the front yard.

"The last load is ready to be taken to the dump, Luke."

"Thanks for your help, fellas, I really appreciate it."

"You guys should come out tonight and shoot a couple games of pool with me," Benny suggested. "Maybe even have a brew or two."

Luke looked from one man to the other, "Carl?"

"Can't. Maggie's cooking a big dinner and then I promised to take her to the movies."

"I think I'll pass too, Benny. I've got a lot of paperwork to catch up on. Maybe another time." Luke didn't really want to go, but he didn't want to come across like he was too good to hang out with his crew after work.

"Come on," Benny pressed. "It's Friday,

you never go out anymore, and besides the paperwork can wait."

Luke knew Benny was right, but he didn't care for the bar scene, especially since he and Pam had split. His mom constantly accused him of being a workaholic, and he had to admit there was some truth to her concern. Maybe it would do him some good to let loose. Besides, it had been a long time since he'd been out and played a game of pool. "Okay, sure. I'll stop by for a little while."

"Great. See you later." Benny waved on his way to the company truck to wait for Carl.

After his two workers left, Luke stared a little longer at the house, knowing there was something special about it. He just didn't know quite what.

Chapter 3

Luke drove his truck into the gravel parking lot of The Drunken Skunk around seven-thirty. It brought back a lot of memories—some good and some bad, but they all had to do with his ex-girlfriend, Pam. They'd met here a few years ago and soon became a serious item, dating for a little over a year. The two of them had danced, fought, and made up inside the four walls he was staring at through his truck's windshield. At least that's how it had been—until the night she left town on the back of a Harley with some guy who was just passing through. Luke never heard from her again.

He'd convinced himself that he'd been in love with her, but he always knew there had been something missing between them.

Shaking off the past, Luke walked up to the door where he was stopped by a bald mountain of muscles checking ID's and collecting the cover charge. After entering the noisy, dimly-lit bar, it took a moment for his eyes to adjust before he spotted Benny over by the pool tables. Luke ordered a beer from a scantily clad waitress in a black tank top that looked at least two sizes too small—no doubt a premeditated decision. The shirt displayed and enhanced her large "store-bought" breasts, a tool of the trade used to garner the maximum amount of tips from the male patrons who became more intoxicated as the night went on.

Through the haze, a group of women were talking and laughing at a table near the dance floor. They caught Luke's attention. When one of them turned around, he recognized her as the beautiful owner of the flower shop, Jordan, and his pulse quickened. He waved, but Jordan's cheerful expression faded. She turned back around to catch the tail end of a joke one of her friends was telling.

Luke didn't understand. Other than catching her when she fell that day, he'd never met her before and couldn't think of any reason for her cold attitude. Was she offended that he'd held her for a moment longer than necessary? The memory of her perfume and the way she'd felt in his arms, caused a strange stirring inside him.

Jordan tried to ignore the fact that Luke was just across the room. She could feel his eyes on her and she didn't like it. She hadn't been out with her girlfriends in ages, so when Megan called Wednesday evening and sounded so excited about all of them getting together, Jordan just didn't have the heart to disappoint her. She'd been sitting home too much lately anyway and a little fun would do her good. That was until Mr. Luke Kincaid showed up and quickened her pulse every time he looked at her. *I'll just ignore him*, she thought, *and maybe he'll go away*. But a nagging feeling in the pit of her stomach told her it probably wouldn't work out quite like she'd hoped.

On the other side of the bar, Luke won the coin toss. "Rack 'em up, Benny."

Glad to oblige, the second man collected the pool balls inside the wooden frame and, with a few flicks of his wrist and two quick shakes, they were in perfect alignment. At just the right spot on the felt, Luke steadied the white cue ball with his index finger and thumb. He picked up the pool cue, leaned over the table, and aimed for the triangular formation.

A loud crack filled the air as the colorful

balls scattered in all directions across the green surface. The solid red rolled into a corner pocket and the blue striped plopped over the edge on one side. Luke chose solids. He and Benny played a couple games, and Luke ordered a second beer.

He didn't drink much and this would be his last for the night. Every so often, he'd glance over at the table where Jordan sat with her friends.

He was intrigued by this woman who'd given him the cold shoulder when he'd ordered the flowers for his mom.

Tonight, the ponytail was gone and her light brown hair cascaded over her shoulders. She was laughing and having a good time.

"Jordan, who's that hot guy that keeps looking over here? Do you know him?" her friend, Lisa inquired. Lisa was one of those people that others just naturally gravitated towards. She was always the life of the party—and constantly on the hunt for her third husband.

"He's just a guy that stopped in the shop the other day, and believe me Lisa, you don't want to get involved with him," Jordan informed her.

"Why not? He's drop-dead gorgeous!" Lisa's eyes lit up like the Christmas tree in Rockefeller Center.

"Trust me," Jordan huffed. "He's not the man for you."

Luke missed a couple of easy shots, and Benny ribbed him about it, but he'd been distracted trying not to stare at Jordan. At the end of the third game, it was do or die time. Luke only needed one shot to win. He walked around to the other side of the pool table, chalked up the cue stick, and leaned over to line up the shot. The smooth wooden cue slid effortlessly under his curved index finger. But just as he was about to shoot, his eyes focused on something in the background. There, right above the blue chalked tip, was Jordan. In that very moment, she turned and glanced toward him, breaking his concentration. He missed the shot he needed to win—a shot he'd have easily made any other time. He swore under his breath as the white cue ball drifted over the edge, falling into the corner pocket.

"Yes!" Benny announced in triumph as his arm made a quick movement up and down, like someone pulling the handle on an old-fashioned slot machine.

Luke congratulated his friend and handed

over a twenty-dollar bill, before placing the cue stick in the rack hanging on the wall. "I think I'm just going to sit and listen to some music for a while before heading home. Thanks for not beating me too bad, Benny. See you Monday morning."

"You got it, Luke," Benny replied, stuffing the money in the front pocket of his jeans.

The band was good. They were playing a mix of rock and roll oldies and country classics. Luke lingered at a small, high-top table, nursing the last of his second beer. A few women tried to get his attention by smiling sweetly as they sashayed by him. Some stared at him as they moved seductively out on the dance floor. Others laughed a little louder than necessary to get him to glance in their direction. Luke was no fool. He knew the game, but he wasn't interested in any of them, at least not tonight.

He felt a tap on his shoulder and when he turned, there stood Amy. She was Carl's oldest daughter and attended college not far from Hilldale. "Hey, Luke. What brings you out tonight?"

"Just a couple games of pool. How about you? How's school?"

Amy was a knock-out—what guys would

call a triple-threat; blonde, blue-eyed, and built. She was a sweetheart. If he'd been a few years younger, and if she wasn't his friend's daughter—Luke's runaway thoughts were interrupted by Amy's answers to his questions.

"School's okay, but I needed to get out with some of my sorority sisters and let my hair down." She giggled and flipped her head.

The sound caught Jordan's attention. She was shocked to see that he was hitting on that...that *girl*. Luke was probably old enough to be her father, well...that might be a slight exaggeration, but still, he was way too old for her. *And what's with that stupid grin on his face?* It looked to Jordan like his dimples were pushed all the way back to his ears. "What a dog," she whispered under her breath.

"Don't get too crazy," Luke warned Amy playfully. "You know how your dad is."

An exaggerated sigh escaped her lips and she nodded her head. They talked a little more, then her head turned toward the band and her eyes lit up. "I love this song! Come dance with me. It'll be fun!" Grabbing Luke's arm, she tugged him onto the dance floor as he protested the whole way.

"You don't want to dance with an old fart like me. Go find yourself a young guy."

"Don't be silly, Uncle Luke. All they want is—" She paused and arched her eyebrows. "Well, you know."

Unfortunately, he did know. Luke tried not to embarrass himself, sticking to moves that were pretty basic. Amy shimmied and shook in her low-cut, tight-fitting outfit, drawing more than a few stares from the other people in the bar. Men and women alike. They danced to a couple more songs before Luke had to call it quits. He wasn't the work-all-day, party-all-night guy he used to be.

Jordan watched as the two made spectacles of themselves. *Luke must really think he's a stud.* Instead of listening to Megan talk about her tyrant of a boss, Jordan kept an eye on him and the blonde hottie as they walked back to his table. They talked a second or two and then hugged. Not like a friendly hug either; it was the full body contact kind. Jordan couldn't believe her eyes.

"Thanks for the dance, Luke." Amy wrapped her arms around his neck, her baby blues softly pleading with him. "And do me a favor, don't tell dad you saw me here tonight, okay? He freaks out over the littlest things."

With that body and those eyes, she could sell snow to an Eskimo. It was a good thing he'd known her since she was a child and was immune to her womanly wiles. "I won't offer the information, Amy, but you know I won't lie to your dad. If he asks me, I'll tell him. Besides, you're not doing anything wrong. You're not drunk and acting all crazy. Do you girls have a designated driver?"

"Of course, we're not idiots, Luke," she said, her tone defensive.

"Good, be careful and study hard. We're all very proud of you."

Placing a kiss on his cheek, Amy reassured him, "I will." At that moment, she looked like the little girl he remembered not that many years ago. "By the way, you should go ask the lady with the brown hair and green shirt to dance. She's been staring at us. I think she likes you, Uncle Luke," she teased, as she walked away.

He shook his head. The female Amy was talking about was Jordan.

The band took a break and Luke went to see how Benny had made out playing pool. They talked about the great shot Benny had made to clinch his last game. His winnings for the night totaled sixty dollars. Luke congratulated him, offering him a rematch some other time.

The music started up again and Luke walked back to his table, but his thoughts drifted to what Amy had said before she left. *Why would Jordan be watching me?* Contrary to what Carl's daughter had implied, Luke was willing to bet Jordan Shaw didn't "like" him.

A few songs later, Luke strolled over to Jordan's table and stopped next to her chair. *Might as well test Amy's theory.* "Good evening, ladies. You all look very lovely tonight."

Her friends acknowledged his compliment with wide smiles and assessing eyes—but not Jordan. He had no business flirting with them. He had a beautiful wife waiting for him at home. She turned and looked up at Luke with a scowl on her face.

"Would you mind if I joined you?" He motioned to the empty chair next to Jordan.

Before she could protest, her friends responded.

"Sure," Megan said, batting her eyelashes.

"You can do anything you want, honey." Lisa winked and stared at him like a fat kid being offered the keys to a candy store.

Three of the four people at the table participated in flirty, bar small talk for a while. The women twittered with laughter at Luke's stories and jokes, but Jordan just rolled her eyes, folded her arms across her chest, and became more irritated with each passing second. An observation on human nature played out before her eyes. *Isn't it strange*, she pondered, *that no matter how old, or how successful and independent a woman is, the mere presence of a handsome man has such an effect on the female behavior*. How had the man sitting next to her transformed her otherwise intelligent and educated friends into giggling, hormone-crazy high school girls?

"Why is there a stuffed skunk behind the bar?" Megan aimed her index finger over her shoulder.

"You've never heard the story of Rosebud and how the bar got its name?" he responded, looking from one woman to the next.

Megan and Lisa shook their heads and turned their full attention toward Luke. Jordan released a frustrated sigh, making sure he understood that she was just tolerating his presence.

"It's a very interesting story, almost a legend around here," he began. "You see when Charlie's dad bought this place, he had to do some repairs before he could open for business, and one of them was to remodel the storeroom. One night he and his buddies were leaving after working all day, and somebody didn't latch the back door. Sometime in the middle of the night, a skunk wandered in looking for something to eat, but all it found were cases of beer.

"Back then, most beer was sold in glass bottles and as the little critter climbed higher in search of a midnight snack, some of the bottles fell and broke. Before long, the skunk realized there wasn't any food to be found, but was curious about the liquid that lay in puddles on the floor.

"It drank the spilled beer, got drunk, and eventually passed out. The next morning when Charlie and his workers got to the bar, they found the animal and the broken bottles of beer."

The women sat captivated like little children listening to their favorite bedtime fairytale.

"Every night after that, the skunk would come around and even though they would secure the storeroom, somehow it always managed to find a way in. Eventually, it became the bar's mascot. Then after a few months,

Charlie showed up one morning and found the little animal dead."

"Oh, poor baby," Lisa responded, dramatically placing her palm flat against her exposed cleavage.

"So Charlie had it stuffed and changed the name of the bar to 'The Drunken Skunk.'"

"Do you really expect us to believe that cockamamie story?" Jordan glared at Luke, leaning her arms on the table in front of her.

"It's the truth, I swear." With his index finger, Luke drew a child-like "x" over his heart, defending the authenticity of the legend. "You can ask Charlie yourself if you don't believe me."

Silence hung in the air for a long minute as Luke and Jordan stared at each other, both experiencing emotions that puzzled yet fascinated them.

In the background, the band started to play one of his favorite songs. He peered over at Jordan, stood and held out his hand. "May I have this dance, Ms. Shaw?" His request was met with a less than enthusiastic response.

"Where's that teeny-bopper you were dancing with earlier?" There was a sarcastic bite in her voice.

"She had to leave."

"Early morning cheerleading practice for homecoming, no doubt." Jordan sneered.

Luke chucked, if he didn't know better, he'd think Jordan was jealous.

"What about the woman you sent those roses to? Won't Anna mind you dancing with other women?" Her tone was cold and accusing.

"I'm sure she wouldn't mind at all."

Jordan saw a look of confusion on his face. Her friends didn't know the story behind the flowers and they prodded her to accept.

"Go for it, Jordan."

"Yeah, you love to dance."

Jordan glared in their direction, her eyes conveying that she didn't want to dance with him and for them to mind their own business. But they persisted. Finally, she scooted her chair back and stood, but didn't take Luke's hand, so he followed her out onto the dance floor. They fell into an easy rhythm and moved well together to an old rock and roll song.

"You're a good dancer, Jordan," Luke said, spinning her around a couple of times.

"Thanks."

"Have I done something to offend you?"

he asked, growing frustrated by her attitude.

"No."

"Then why the cold shoulder?"

"Isn't it obvious?" She responded with a sharpness in her voice. "Why does it matter anyway?"

"I just wanted to know why a beautiful woman like you is—"

"Is what?" Jordan interrupted, her brows furrowed as she readied herself to confront him and his lame pickup line. "Not swooning over you and falling at your feet like my friends and the young blonde?"

A smirk twitched at his lips. "What I was going to say was, 'Why is it that a beautiful woman like you doesn't smile more often?'"

Jordan didn't answer, wondering what his motives might be for all the attention he was giving her. Was he after conquests? Was he a chronic cheater just out for the thrill of the hunt? The song ended and she searched his deep brown eyes. The expression she saw sent the same heat rushing through her that she'd experienced in the flower shop that day.

Taking a step back, she attempted to return to her friends. Just then a slow, classic oldie started and Luke reached for her hand. Even though her heart insisted she give in and her body longed to be close to him again, Jordan hesitated. She knew she should run from the dangers that came with getting involved with such a handsome man—especially a married one. But the temptation to be close to him was just too strong for her to resist.

Luke drew Jordan to him and, with his palm flat against her back, pressed her close. Her body molded perfectly to his. At that moment, they were the only two people on the dance floor. The music became muffled, like the whistle of a distant train. As they swayed to the rhythm of the song, he breathed in the light, fresh scent of Jordan's perfume. It reminded him of a warm spring morning with the sun shining down on a field of wildflowers.

Wrapped in Luke's strong, muscular arms, Jordan's pulse quickened and her legs grew weak. She'd noticed his body that day at the shop when he'd caught her. But now, up against him like this, it left little to the imagination. Closing her eyes, she let herself be carried away by the soft melody and was soon lost in Luke's embrace.

It had been such a long time since a man had held her like this. She'd forgotten how good it felt. The musky smell of his cologne drifted around her and caused a wave of sensations in the pit of her stomach. There was an unexplainable force pulling her towards him. When the song ended, they eased apart and their eyes locked. Jordan's heart missed a beat when she saw the smoldering desire in Luke's eyes. Did hers reflect the undeniable longing to be back in his arms that she felt powerless to hide?

Just then, the image of the beautiful woman she'd delivered flowers to popped into her head, along with what he'd written on the card. Her eyes grew hard. She pushed away from him, leaving him stunned and standing in the middle of the dance floor. She hurried back to the table where Lisa and Megan sat, green with envy, wishing *they* had been the ones wrapped in his arms.

Making his way through the crowd, Luke followed her. "What was that?"

"Nothing. The song was over, that's all," she informed him bluntly, avoiding eye contact, knowing she couldn't say what needed to be said if she were gazing into his handsome face.

After an awkward moment, Luke smiled politely. "Well, thank you for the dance, Jordan. Maybe we could do it again sometime."

"I don't think so, Mr. Kincaid. No matter what you say, I'm positive that Anna wouldn't think that was a good idea at all. Now goodnight." The legs of Jordan's chair scraped on concrete floor as she stood and marched toward the restroom, leaving Luke standing alone once again, rejected and confused.

Luke glanced at the other two women at the table and nodded. "Have a good night, ladies." Then, pulling his keys from the front pocket of his jeans, he turned and left the bar.

When Jordan returned to the table, Lisa was the first to start the interrogation. "Why were you so rude to that sexy guy? He was the best-looking piece of eye candy in this place. What's wrong with you?"

"Nothing," Jordan snapped. "Just drop it. I'm in no mood to discuss Mr. Luke Kincaid." Images of the handsome men from her past flashed in Jordan's mind. Both had hurt her deeply, and she wasn't about to let it happen again. Her past had taught her a valuable lesson. Males like Luke were trouble. They couldn't be trusted, and it would do her well not to forget that.

So why, at that very moment, did her body

flush with heat and start to tingle, reminding her how good it had felt wrapped in his arms while they were dancing.

Chapter 4

Luke woke up early Saturday morning. He hadn't slept very well. The events of last night plagued his thoughts. Jordan was beautiful, and he felt overwhelmingly drawn to her. She, on the other hand, certainly didn't think much of him. Although, there was that moment on the dance floor when he saw a momentary glimpse of something warm in her eyes. He liked holding her, like that first time at her flower shop. Just then his chest tightened, confirming a fact he was becoming rapidly aware of—Jordan Shaw was someone special.

Luke arrived at the old house around seven o'clock. A cool breeze ruffled his hair as he crossed the driveway on his way to the porch. He paused for a moment to admire the intricate design on the etched oval window in the center of the front door.

The air inside smelled musty like a house too long ignored by soap and water. Luke coughed and sneezed a few times as his body reacted to the dust that floated and danced in the beams of sunlight. Cobwebs hung like delicate lace across every corner of the room, glistening eerily in the filtered rays of the sun. Enough light shone through the dirty, cracked windowpanes that he didn't need his flashlight—at least for the tasks he wanted to do today. He opened all the windows and doors so the fresh morning air could flow through the main level of the house.

The old pine floors needed refinishing. Scuff and scrape marks from moving heavy furniture around were most evident in what had probably been the living room. There was a dark spot on the wood in front of the oversized picture window. Maybe from a plant that had been given too much to drink, causing its container to leak and drip, damaging and discoloring the floor. A board creaked here and there as Luke's work boots traveled from room to room. But over all, it looked to be in fairly good condition. Nothing seemed to be rotting through and none of the boards were missing. As he continued his inspection, Luke saw evidence that mice had found their way inside to nest and hide from the feral cats and owls that lived in the trees behind the house. He'd have to hire someone to come out and get rid of them. Also, he'd have them spray the entire place for other unwanted pests.

He wanted to renovate all the bathrooms, maybe even add a couple extra. Every window in the house would need to be replaced with more energy efficient ones, and the old wiring and plumbing would need to be brought up to code. The back porch was the same size as the one at the front of the house. It looked out onto a large yard bordered by a thick grove of towering oaks and pines. They provided much needed shade against summer's blazing, afternoon heat, along with protection from winter's frigid, blowing winds and spring's pelting rains.

There were a lot of things on his to-do list that he hoped to accomplish today. It was going to be a time-consuming and labor-intensive remodeling job, but the bones of the house were good. He loved restoring life back into something others had given up for worthless. Working with his hands gave him a sense of pride and satisfaction when, in the end, he could stand back and look at the completed project.

Working steadily, Luke cleaned the sizable stone fireplace that occupied most of one wall in the living room. After removing the years of dirt and soot, he was pleased to find the mortar still in good shape. Using his flashlight, he checked to see if birds had taken up residence in the chimney. He wasn't surprised to find the opening was indeed blocked. He made a note to call Gene Porter on Monday morning and schedule an appointment for him to come and clean it out. He was the only person in town that Luke knew who could handle the job.

Next, he began to tear down the wall that separated the dining room from the living room. His plan was to turn the two smaller rooms into one breathtaking great room that welcomed guests as they entered the house. Several layers of wallpaper in various colors and designs covered both sides of the wall. Brittle with age and peeling away at the seams, they sometimes crumbled in his hands. By the time he finished pulling down the sheet rock, a film of fine dust covered his clothes and any exposed skin. The breeze had stopped and left the house stuffy. Luke's shirt and hair were soaked with sweat. When it mixed with the dirt and the chalky powder from the drywall, little streaks of mocha-colored moisture ran down his arms, face, and neck.

He made several trips out to the bed of his truck hauling the rubble created by his hours of manual labor. Luke swept the floor and then stood back to survey what he'd been able to get done so far. On his way outside to wash off some of the sweat and change into a dry shirt, he stopped suddenly. Out of the corner of his eye, he caught a glimpse of something stuck in the wall near the floor. Walking over to investigate, he reached down and pulled out a dusty, brown leather book that had been wedged and partially hidden between two studs.

"How in the hell did *this* get in the wall?" he muttered. Luke wiped his hands the best he could on the cleanest dirty spot of his jeans. Turning the book over, he noticed a word embossed on the front of it. Even though the gold letters were worn and scratched, he could still read it: *JOURNAL*.

Luke eased opened the book. The pages were stiff and yellow, the binding crackled from age and lack of use. Inside the front cover was an inscription written in perfect penmanship by a woman's delicate hand:

To M.J.
For all of your private thoughts.
Happy 18th Birthday!
Love,
Mother and Dad

It was just the diary of a teenage girl from long ago. Nothing important. Nothing valuable. He'd toss it in with the rest of the trash to haul away.

Later when he walked outside to add the diary to the pile in the back of his truck, he hesitated. Something stirred deep inside him. Luke tossed it on the front seat instead. Maybe his mom or sister-in-law would enjoy reading the old book.

He attached a garden hose to the faucet on the side of the house and proceeded to clean up before taking a break for lunch. After finishing the tasks he'd planned for that day, Luke unloaded his truck at the dump then headed home. He was tired and ready for a hot shower. While relaxing on the couch, he flipped through the TV channels, catching the last few innings of a baseball game between two of his favorite teams before going to bed.

The journal stayed in Luke's truck for several days. He thought he should clean it up a little first before giving it to Anna. Taking it inside one night, he set it on the kitchen table, where it sat for over a week.

Tuesday night after work, there wasn't anything on television worth watching, and he was bored. He went into the kitchen to see what his options were for dinner, and there on the table was the dusty journal, right where he'd left it. Taking a damp towel, he carefully wiped off the brown leather cover. Luke started to wonder if there might be something written inside about anyone he knew. He chuckled at the idea, so he carried it back into the living room, deciding to satisfy his curiosity.

Not wanting to dislodge any of the brittle pages, he opened the book slowly and read the first entry written in the dainty and flowing pen stokes of the young girl.

What a glorious day this has been! The birthday party was wonderful! My friends and family were all here. Mother out did herself and the food was delicious. And that cake! Oh my goodness, it looked like something that would have been served at a beautiful wedding. But the best part was that

Brad was here! He surprised me by proposing!! Of course, I cried and said yes! I love him so very much! I can't wait to become his wife and spend the rest of our lives together. People say we're too young, but I know that we'll have the perfect life! I'm still so excited, I doubt I'll be able to sleep a wink tonight.

Rolling his eyes at the youthful ramblings of the teenager who wrote it, he knew this was definitely more suited to a female's taste, not his. With a huff, he laid it on the coffee table in front of him.

Later that night, Luke fell asleep with thoughts of Jordan running through his mind. Vivid memories of the dances they'd shared, her body pressed up against his, and those fleeting few seconds when her aqua eyes were soft and tender as they gazed up at him.

Two more weeks went by, and he still hadn't found time to the take the diary to his mother.

There was something about that old, brown leather, book. Every day when he walked past it, he felt more and more drawn to it. Each night after work, just before going to sleep, he read an entry or two from the journal.

He couldn't seem to hand it over to Audra and Anna just yet. The story of M.J. began to intrigue him. He found himself being pulled in by her words.

I got a letter from Brad today and he sent a picture of himself in his uniform. He looks so handsome! I'm the luckiest girl in the world and all my friends are jealous. He can't tell me where he is exactly, but I pray every night for his safety. Mother and I have started looking through magazines and in the local stores for items for the wedding. We haven't bought much yet since I have no idea when Brad will be home. I hear my obnoxious little brother, A.J., outside in the hall, so I'll have to write more later. I hide my journal in the old vent so he won't find it and read it. He is such a pest! Sometimes I wish I were an only child.

Luke started to have dreams about this girl and how she might have looked. He'd read about her wedding plans and how Brad planned to work at his father's law firm after he came home.

How he'd joined the military and been sent overseas to fight in the war. How proud she was of him, and how she missed him and looked forward to his letters. One night as he turned to the next entry, he noticed something looked different.

The handwriting was shaky and harder to read. Soon the reason became clear.

> *Today my life was turned upside down. Two men in military uniforms came to the house and informed me that Brad was wounded in action. He will be coming back home next week. But they wouldn't tell me any of the details regarding his injuries, and I'm not sure I truly want to know. I'm so worried about him! What if he dies? What will I do then?*

Luke noticed there were spots that looked like splattered droplets of water on the page, blurring some of the letters. He believed they were M.J.'s tears.

A few nights later, he'd read in the journal about one of her visits with Brad.

I went to see Brad in the hospital today. He looked so different, he was pale and thin. He wasn't happy I was there. He said he didn't want my pity, and even though I tried to convince him how much I still love him and I only want to be there for him, he refused to believe me. He yelled hateful things at me, so I left in tears. A few hours later, he called and apologized, but I know something is terribly wrong. I worry that he has been through too much to ever fully return to the man he was.

His heart went out to this woman he'd never met and the pain she'd gone through.

As he slept that night, dreams of the broken-hearted girl roamed through Luke's mind. He'd come to know her these last couple of weeks and found himself looking forward to hearing about the life she'd planned with Brad. Luke became aware that he wanted to protect her from the cards life had dealt her at such a young age. A part of him wished he could reach back in time and comfort her, letting her know that everything would be all right.

But who was he to think he could offer her consolation or make such a promise.

There was another woman competing for time in his dreams—the pretty florist. He couldn't stop thinking about how good it had felt to hold her in his arms that night at the bar...and how he longed to hold her again.

Chapter 5

It was Saturday and the annual Chamber of Commerce Charity Auction was tonight. The proceeds were going to the Make a Wish Foundation this year. Luke didn't particularly like wearing his one and only suit, let alone a tie, but it was a formal event, and he didn't want to bother renting a tux. The bright side was that he was confident Jordan would be there. He'd seen her name on the list of businesses scheduled to participate. The event was a silent auction. The whole town was invited to bid on the items and services that had been donated by local merchants; including the radio and television stations.

Even though cocktails had started at six o'clock, Luke didn't arrive at the convention center until a few minutes before seven. After straightening his black suit jacket, he tugged at the neckline of his light blue dress shirt with his index finger one last time, before walking into the spacious, but already crowded, room. A dozen or so people gathered near the bar. Several others mingled in small groups here and there laughing and talking about topics that ranged from politics to recipes. Men slapped each other on the back when one of their buddies delivered the punch line to a new dirty joke. Hushed gasps and whispers came from other sections as they traded the latest and juiciest gossip, unconcerned with its validity.

Certain wealthy, tuxedo-clad men and their much younger trophy wives came dressed to impress. Dripping with sparkling diamond accessories, the women wore expensive, flowing gowns from all the latest designers. With a calculated effort to make their presence known, the couples hobnobbed from one group of movers-and-shakers to another. Bursts of insincere, but socially-expected laughter rose from the small clusters of the high society elite.

A local band played quietly in the background. Strings of small, shimmering, white lights, like the ones used at Christmastime or at weddings, hung from the ceiling. They draped in swags from one side of the room to the other creating a festive but elegant mood.

One by one, people took the time to stroll down the rows of tables covered with black linens, perusing the items up for bid. All the guests received a number when walking inside tonight. They were to use it when writing their bids on the sheets of paper next to each entry instead of using their names. This enhanced the fun by keeping the bidder's identity a secret until the winners were announced at the end of the evening.

Luke stood just inside the door while his eyes skimmed the crowd for one particular person. He spotted Jordan talking to the woman who owned the tanning salon a few doors down from her flower shop—and a good-looking man that he didn't recognize. Jordan looked amazing in a red strapless dress that hugged her body. Her shiny, light mocha-colored hair lay in loose curls over her bare shoulders and back. She may not have the stereotypical body-type of a Hooter's waitress, but at the sight of her, Luke had to remind himself to breathe.

Jordan must have felt his stare because she turned, and when her eyes met his, the corners of her mouth drooped. Her lips formed a straight, thin line across her face. Before she returned her attention to the conversation around her, Luke caught her gaze sweep over him, from top to bottom. But her expression gave nothing away. He really wanted to know what he'd done to receive the cold shoulder treatment and wondered if the man standing way too close to Jordan was her date. He hoped not. A spark of reality stopped him. He had no right to be jealous. She'd never given him any reason to think she was interested in him—even a little. So why couldn't he stop glancing over at her every few minutes, wishing that he was the one standing next to her, making her smile, making her laugh.

It had been a busy week for Jordan. Proms for both of the local high schools had been held last night. She'd also had to deliver flowers for a wedding this morning. But thankfully, it wasn't a large affair and Darcy had been a big help with the corsages and boutonnieres, leaving Jordan free to work on the bouquet and larger arrangements.

Jordan enjoyed community events like this one, especially since it helped deserving kids. Plus it gave her a chance to get dressed up and talk to people she didn't see that often. When she turned and saw Luke staring at her, she hadn't anticipated her body's reaction to seeing him dressed in a suit. He looked dashingly handsome. Her heart raced in her chest. He was sexy enough in his jeans and work shirt, but tonight, he could've easily stepped off the cover of GQ.

Jordan knew that she had to avoid any situation where she'd have to make polite conversation with him, because as much as her body wanted to be near him, her brain reminded her that he was married. No matter how good-looking and charming he might be, she remembered all too well the pain on her mother's face after finding out the truth about her father. Jordan refused to be "the other woman."

After making the rounds and socializing with a few other people, Jordan and Andy strolled toward the long row of tables to review the items available. "What are you going to bid on, Sis?" he asked.

"Um, definitely the car repair to use for the delivery van in case it breaks down."

"Wow, you really know how to live it up, don't you?" he teased. "Why don't you bid on something fun instead of practical? Like maybe this spa package or this cruise."

Placing one hand on her hip, Jordan playfully responded, "Because, little brother, I *need* this and I don't *need* either of those." As the pair proceeded down the row of display tables, Jordan was pleased to see several bids for her donation.

"So what did you contribute?" Andy caught up to her after becoming sidetracked reading the details of a ski trip package. He smiled with pride knowing that his company could've offered a better experience for less money.

"The winner will get to choose from a couple of options as long as what they want falls within the price range I've agreed to donate. That seems to be the way most people prefer to bid on items at events like this."

Her brother just nodded and continued down the table. "This is what you *need* right here," tapping his index finger on the sheet of paper in front of him. Jordan walked over to see what he was pointing at and her heart stopped. It was Luke's donation. "You need a deck out in the backyard. We could have some awesome barbeques and parties out there. How about a shed to store all your overflow supplies? You really should bid on this."

Jordan stared down at the paper, but didn't respond with the same enthusiasm as he did. "No. I...ah...I think I'll pass. I'm sure it will

go for way more than I'm willing to spend."
Her voice cracked slightly and her hands
started to shake. She prayed Andy hadn't noticed.

"Oh come on, there's not that many bids
yet, and I know you can afford it," he prodded. "Besides, if you choose the storage shed
for the shop, you can write it off on your tax-
es."

There was no way she could bid on
Luke's item. She was too attracted to him and
knew she couldn't spend that much time
around him. Trying to act as if she wasn't interested without having to explain why, she
just shrugged, "Nah, I don't think so. But,
you were right about bidding on something
just for fun, just for me." Jordan walked back
down the row of tables, placing a bid on the
spa package. "I could use a nice massage every now and then."

While his sister was busy at the other end
of the table, Andy quickly wrote her bidding
number down for Luke's item, along with a
sizable dollar amount. After looking at everything that had been donated, Andy went back
and bid on the cruise for himself.

The lights started to dim and someone announced that dinner was about to be served.

Jordan and her brother made their way to one of the many round tables set in the middle of the room. The crisp, white-linen napkins popped against the black tablecloths, the same fabric that was used for the display tables. Beautiful, silk floral arrangements created with different sizes and shapes of white flowers with sprigs of greenery decorated the center of each table. Each one wrapped around a glass hurricane-shaped vase containing a tall white candle that cast a pleasant glow out into the room.

Jordan breathed a sigh of relief when she discovered that her friends had saved the last two seats at their table for her and Andy. At least she'd be able to eat in peace knowing that Luke Kincaid wouldn't be able to sit next to her.

Over the course of the evening, Luke caught glimpses of Jordan and was disappointed he hadn't had a chance to talk to her yet. Noticing there was no more room at her table, he took a seat at another one not far from her. Now he'd have to wait to find out more about her—and that guy she was with.

All through dinner, Jordan avoided looking in Luke's direction as much as possible, stealing only a peek or two. She didn't like the jittery feeling her body experienced when she was near him. The meal was almost over when she heard a burst of hearty laughter coming from a nearby table. When she looked over, there was the pair of twinkling brown eyes and sexy smile she'd tried to avoid all night. Luke raised his glass in her direction and winked. Disturbing sensations spiraled through her body. She had just taken the last bite of her dessert when an involuntary gasp attempted to escape down her throat, causing her to choke and cough.

"Sis? Are you okay?" Andy gently patted her back. "Here, take a drink of water."

Even though she was embarrassed, she waved away the concerned looks that showed on the faces of her friends as she tried to stop the spasms in her throat. After a moment, she was finally able to speak. "Sorry everyone—I guess," she paused to cough. "That last bite— must've gone down—the wrong way." She could feel her face flush with heat as she took another drink of water.

"You sure you're okay?" Andy whispered.

She nodded her head. "I think I'll just run to the ladies room and freshen up. I'll only be a minute." Scooting her chair back, she excused herself, and with all the dignity she could gather, she walked across the room and out into the wide hallway.

Staring at her reflection in the bathroom mirror, she was thankful to see that her eye shadow and mascara hadn't left streaks down her face. Taking a moment to touch up her foundation and lipstick, Jordan closed her eyes remembering the look Luke had given her. The waves of tingling heat took hold again. What was it about the man that caused her body to react the way it did? What was it that attracted her to men that were no good for her? With a slow, deep breath, she decided it was time to head back to the party before her friends and Andy began to worry about her.

Not long after Jordan left, Luke's cell phone vibrated in his pocket. He excused himself from the group of people he'd been talking with and stepped through the double doors to get away from the noise. "Hello."

"Hi, Luke," a female's velvety voice tickled his ear. "Are you busy?"

"Not really. I'm at the charity auction I told you about."

"Oh my, I'm so sorry to interrupt. I'll call you back tomorrow."

The southern charm of his sister-in-law

was a pleasant distraction. "No, it's fine, Audra. We've just finished dinner. What's up?"

"I wanted to ask if you'd have time to drive me to the airport next week. I fly out on Wednesday morning."

"Of course I will. What time should I pick you up?"

"Nine o'clock should give me enough time. My flight leaves at eleven-thirty."

"Okay, I'll see you then." Luke made a mental note to put it on the planner in his phone as soon as they hung up so it would remind him that morning.

"Thank you so much, you're a dear," she said, her unmistakable drawl emphasizing the last couple of words.

They said their goodbyes and he chuckled to himself. Audra was one hundred percent southern belle.

Just as she stepped out of the ladies room, Jordan noticed Luke talking on his cell phone. By the way he was smiling, she had no doubt that there was a female on the other end of the call. *I wonder if he's talking to Anna—or another woman.* Maybe if she was careful, she could slip back into the banquet room without him seeing her. No such luck. Halfway across the large hallway, Luke's call ended and when he turned, his eyes locked onto hers. The distance between them soon disappeared with every stride of his muscular legs.

"Are you all right, Jordan?" His deep voice caused a shiver to race down her spine.

Jordan glared up at the face she wished didn't affect her so. "Well, I hope you're happy, Mr. Kincaid!"

Luke's eyes narrowed and he frowned. "What are you talking about?"

With her hands firmly planted on her hips, Jordan took a step in his direction. "I was very embarrassed in there, and it's all your fault."

His eyebrows arched at the unexpected accusation, "How is it *my* fault?"

"Don't play dumb with me!" she snapped. "You guys are all alike with your charming little grins and flirty eye twitches." She demonstrated, exaggerating blinking movements with one eye to prove her point.

Luke tried to control the smirk that threatened to form on his lips. "I see you've found us out. Yes, we men have set out to rule the world and ruin the lives of all women with a smile and a wink as our devious weapons of mass destruction." Unable to stop himself, he burst out laughing at the absurdity of what she was implying. He thought humor would help defuse the situation—but it didn't.

"You think this is funny?" she barked. "I was mortified in there!" She flung her arm in the direction of the banquet room for emphasis. "And you're the one who caused it! How dare you stand here and laugh at me!"

"Do you hear yourself, Jordan? I'm sorry you choked, but it's not my fault. I'm glad you're feeling better. I just don't understand why you insist on blaming me?"

Jordan suddenly realized that she was sounding somewhat irrational about the whole thing, but she couldn't back down now. Poking her index finger in his chest, she explained. "If you hadn't been here tonight, none of this would've happened. That's why it's your fault, Mr. Kincaid! And by the way, where is Anna tonight? Shouldn't she be here with you?" Not waiting for an answer, Jordan turned and marched back into the charity event, her head held high as her spiky heels clicked on the tile floor.

Luke stood there a few more minutes, frustrated that every time he spoke with Jordan, things got worse between them. He was sincerely sorry about what happened and wanted her to know that he was concerned about her. But all that got him was a lecture on the sinister plans of the male species. And why was she always so concerned about his mother? As far as he knew, they'd never met, yet this was the second time Jordan had asked about her—once at the bar and now again tonight. Puzzled by his encounter with Jordan, he shook his head and returned to his table joining in the conversations around him as if nothing had happened. Yet he couldn't stop thinking about the lovely woman just a few feet away.

Half an hour later, the Mayor stepped onto the stage and tapped on the microphone with his index finger, testing to see if it was turned on. He gave a short speech, thanking everyone for coming and for the generous participation in tonight's event. "Now, let's get down to business and announce the winners of these wonderful donations."

The applause died down and he went through the list of items, reading the name of the person who had placed the highest bid. Luke's name was announced as the winner of the auto repair. Mrs. Merriweather won Jordan's entry. Andy was bummed he'd been outbid for the cruise.

"This next item was donated by Kincaid Construction."

Jordan refused to look in Luke's direction and focused her eyes down on the table in front of her. "And the highest bidder is...Ms. Jordan Shaw." Her head snapped toward the stage and every muscle in her body tensed. She knew there had to be a mistake. She hadn't placed a bid on his donation. Just as she was about to protest, she felt a warm hand on her arm.

"Surprise!" Andy beamed, proud that he'd pulled one over on his big sister. Jordan stared at him with a look on her face that he hadn't seen since they were kids, but recognized immediately—Mt. St. Jordan was about to blow.

"Why did you do that? Are you crazy?" she demanded quietly through gritted teeth as she glared at him.

"What?" Andy had known there was a good chance she'd be unhappy with him at first, but he hadn't expected her to respond quite like this. "Why are you so upset?"

Jordan didn't want to go into the reason, especially with her little brother. She exhaled deeply and shook her head, "Never mind. You just shouldn't have done that."

Andy knew better than that and pressed for an answer. "Spill it, Sis. What's the real deal?"

"Nothing. I guess I'm just tired." She leaned over and lightly kissed his cheek. "Thanks."

Following the announcement, Jordan couldn't bring herself to look at Luke. He must be enjoying every minute of this after her tirade earlier.

Luke was confused, but glad, now he'd get to spend more time with her—alone. Once all the winners had been announced, several people said their goodbye's, calling it a night.

The remainder either gathered at the bar or milled around the room in small groups discussing the evening. Remembering the shocked and angry reaction on Jordan's face when the mayor called her name, Luke noticed that the man next to her had looked a little too pleased with himself.

"I'm surprised that you bid on my donation," he admitted as he approached Jordan.

"That makes two of us," she mumbled.

"Excuse me?"

Before Jordan could explain, Andy joined them and draped his arm around Jordan's bare shoulders. Luke gave her a questioning look then focused his attention back on the man standing next to her.

"I don't believe we've met, I'm Luke Kincaid. I was just talking with Jordan about my donation that she won."

Removing his arm from around his sister, he offered his hand. "Nice to meet you. I'm Andy, Jordan's brother." He glanced over at her. "She's not real happy with me right now because I'm the one that actually placed the bid for her."

Brother? Luke was relieved to find out that this guy was someone she wasn't romantically involved with. He looked at Jordan. "So—you didn't—"

She shook her head. "I apologize for my brother's idea of fun. I'm sure if I talk to the committee chairman we can find out who the next highest bidder was and they can take advantage of your services."

A sly twitch played on Luke's mouth. "Why? Don't you *need* any of my services?"

Jordan's mouth went dry, well aware of the double meaning in his question.

"See? That's the problem," Andy chimed in, totally clueless. "She could definitely benefit from a shed in her backyard, but for some reason, she thinks what I did was awful and underhanded."

Jordan's face grew hot imagining things she shouldn't and wishing her brother would just shut up.

Amused by the color that appeared on her face, Luke knew she'd understood his teasing. "Okay, well that settles it. I'll call you at the shop next week to discuss the details and find out when it will be convenient for me to start."

He stared at Jordan, a spark of victory reflecting in his eyes. She looked from one man to the other and her shoulders sagged in defeat. "Fine. At least you'll be outside and not in my way. Maybe we could schedule it for July and August. Your macho act won't be so charming and funny when you're about to pass out from heat stroke," she snarled before she turned and walked away. Regardless of whether or not she needed the shed, she didn't want Luke working at her house when she wasn't there. He'd be coming on Saturday, which meant she'd have to take those days off. And Saturday was her busiest day. She rubbed her temple. *I could always call Helen. She's reliable and I trust her to run the shop.*

Luke looked to Andy for some answers to his sister's behavior, but all he received was a shrug and a pat on the shoulder, "Good luck, buddy, you're gonna need it."

Jordan had to avoid spending any more time around Luke. His deep voice and dazzling smile did strange things to her. They could make a girl dream of romance, lace, and moon lit nights. Those notions were best left to the ignorant young and foolish dreamers. Jordan dared not believe in those kinds of dreams. Being near him was too dangerous and she wouldn't take the chance that something might happen—something that she'd regret for the rest of her life.

Andy returned to their table after talking to a pretty woman he'd seen across the room. "So are you still mad, Sis?"

Jordan knew he'd done it for the right reasons, but it still annoyed her. "I just can't believe you'd do something like that behind my back."

"Oh, calm down, it's not that big a deal. So a good-looking guy, that I'd bet you have a crush on by the way you're acting, comes to your house for a few weekends. What's the problem?"

Glaring at her brother, she tried to explain.

"The problem is...well, I just don't..." Jordan paused. But seeing the smirk on Andy's face at her failed attempt to justify her protests, she corrected him. "And for your information, I do not have a *crush* on Luke Kincaid."

Andy shook his head. "Some things never change. You're still a drama queen, M.J." Jordan's face lost all its color. "Hey, Sis. Are you okay?"

An icy wave of panic rushed through her. A lump formed in her throat. With a steely glare aimed at her brother, her hand gripped his arm like a vise. "Don't ever call me that!" she whispered just inches from his face, her tone rough and angry. She immediately scanned the area around them to see if anyone could have overheard Andy's unfortunate slip of the tongue. "Don't call me that in public! I can't afford for the scandal to re-surface. I'd lose everything."

He'd seen that look before and instinct told him to just nod, communicating the fact that he'd gotten the message—loud and clear.

Chapter 6

Over a late lunch on Sunday afternoon, Luke was talking to his mother and Audra about how well the business was doing. He wanted Anna to be proud that he'd taken his dad's company and continued to expand it and grow its reputation, as well as its net worth.

"You work too much, son," she scolded.

"I need to. We have lots of jobs on the schedule. I've even had to turn some work away."

"What about a social life?" Audra's tone was filled with love and concern as she gazed at her brother-in-law.

"I'm just too busy right now, and when I'm not working, I'm too tired to chase women," he said with a chuckle, only half-kidding.

"You need to find a nice girl and settle down." Anna wasn't about to let him off that easy. "Life's too short to waste it all working.

Besides, you're not getting any younger, dear."

"Gee, thanks." Luke shook his head, but at that moment, Jordan's face popped into his mind. *Odd timing*, he thought, while images of her tugged at the pit of his stomach.

She reached over and lovingly patted his arm. "I just want you to be happy and not have any regrets later."

Audra smiled in his direction. "You're a good man, Luke. You'd be a great catch for some lucky woman."

"Work will slow down in a few months when the weather turns cold, and I'll be able to relax a little. Maybe then I'll give some thought to going in search of another daughter-in-law for you." He winked at his mother.

Wednesday morning, Luke's phone beeped, reminding him that it was time to pick up Audra from his mom's house and drive her to the airport. When he walked in, his sister-in-law's suitcases were waiting by the door, and he heard female voices coming from the kitchen.

"I'm so glad you came and spent some time with me. I wish the two of you didn't live so far away." Anna hugged her daughter-in-law.

"I had a wonderful visit. Philip is trying to get a transfer with his company to this area, but so far, there aren't any openings. I know he wants to be closer to you, too."

Anna saw a hint of sadness in the younger woman's hazel eyes. "I guess I'm being selfish, I'm sorry. Moving here would take you away from all of *your* friends and family."

Audra paused. "That's true, but my parents are planning to retire in the next year or so. They are going to travel for a while before settling down in Florida. It wouldn't be the same back home without them there."

Luke carried the luggage out to the truck while the two women finished their goodbyes. Audra's shoes clicked on the cement walkway as she made her way to where Luke was waiting. He didn't understand her choice of clothes for the long flight, a designer dress and three-inch heels. Her hair and make-up were impeccable, as usual. She looked more like she was going out to a nice dinner instead of getting ready to spend the next several hours stuck on a plane.

With one last wave, Luke and Audra headed for the airport. "I appreciate you taking time from work to drive me. I hope it isn't too much trouble. I could've called a taxi."

"Don't worry about it, that's what family's for." He tossed her a playful smile. "Besides, my brother would have my hide if I'd let some stranger in a stinky cab take you anywhere."

Audra smothered a giggle and nodded in agreement at her brother-in-law's statement regarding her over-protective husband.

Jordan checked her watch again. She was running late to meet Andy's flight. Even though he was just here a couple of weeks ago, he was coming out to visit her again. He'd scheduled a few appointments in order to promote his company with some of the ski resorts and other businesses that catered to his type of clientele in the areas near Hood River. After driving around a few minutes, she finally found an empty parking spot and slid her SUV into the space.

She hurried across the lot then dodged through the street traffic. She was about to enter the automatic doors when she spotted a couple hugging on the sidewalk a few feet away. The woman turned slightly and Jordan recognized her as the beautiful woman with auburn hair whom she'd delivered flowers to a few weeks ago.

Then, the man next to her stepped away

and Jordan's heart tightened—it was Luke Kincaid.

"Have a safe trip and don't forget to call Anna when you get home, you know how she worries," Luke reminded her.

"I will." Audra kissed his cheek and thanked him again for giving her a ride to the airport.

Jordan could hear them talking, but couldn't make out what was being said. With her heart pounding, she rushed through the glass doors and found a seat in the waiting area near the security checkpoint where Andy would be sure to see her. Taking a deep breath, she willed her pulse to return to a more normal speed. Jordan didn't understand why the sight of Luke showing affection to the stunning woman outside should have taken her by surprise. After all, he was her husband.

"Sis?" A male voice interrupted her thoughts. Suddenly the area around her had filled up with people where moments ago she had been one of only three or four.

"Hi, Andy." She greeted her little brother with a quick hug. "I'm glad to see you."

He squinted at her. "You seemed preoccupied just now. Is everything all right?"

Jordan waved off his question. "It's nothing, just business," she lied. "Are you hungry?"

Andy laughed as their steps fell into a rhythm together. "Duh, of course I am. That was a silly question."

"You're right, I should've known better," Jordan agreed. "Where do you want to go?"

Both eyebrows raised on her brother's face, indicating that Jordan had asked another dumb question, one that she should already know the answer to. She glanced down at her watch. "This early? Really?"

Andy responded with a wide grin and a shake of his head.

Jordan gave him a playful shove. "Okay, Burger Barn it is." They both laughed out loud as they strolled through the crowded airport.

Luke was meeting his mom and one of her friends for dinner Friday night at the Ironwood Steakhouse. They had the best tasting T-bones in town and his taste buds had been looking forward to enjoying one all week. The place was rustic, but not hokey. A little sawdust was scattered across the floor and mixed with the peanut shells the customers were encouraged to toss down there.

He hadn't been waiting long before a young woman in a yellow dress approached the table. "Excuse me. Are you Luke?"

Remembering the manners drilled into him by his father, he stood and extended his hand. He didn't recognize her, but nodded in answer to her question. She was pretty, but not so much that she'd stand out in a crowd. Her figure was what people would call hourglass, a little fuller in the bust and hips, but narrower at the waist.

"I'm Valerie, Anna's friend," she explained.

Luke hoped his expression didn't reveal what he was thinking. He'd expected a woman closer to his mother's age to join them. Anna was up to something—and that wasn't good. He motioned to one of the empty chairs. "Please, have a seat." After a slight pause, he continued. "How do you know my mother?"

"We're on the hospital fund raising committee together." The way Valerie was staring at him, Luke felt as if he'd just become the house special on tonight's menu.

No, he thought, *this is not going to turn out well*. Waiting for his mom to join them, he did his best to make polite conversation. Suddenly his cell phone buzzed. "Excuse me," he said, reaching into his pants pocket. It was a text message—from his mother. *Sorry son, something has come up at the last minute and I won't be able to make dinner tonight. I hope you have a nice time with Valerie. She's a sweet lady, so behave. Love you.*

Under the circumstances, Luke knew there was nothing he could do about it now. Tonight had been a set-up. He should have guessed as much after the talk they'd had the other day.

"Is something wrong?" his "date" asked.

"Um, not exactly. Anna won't be joining us tonight after all."

"Oh, that's too bad," Valerie muttered

She doesn't look all that sorry. I wonder if she's in cahoots with Anna on tonight's plan. Probably not, she looked genuinely surprised when I told her we are going to be dining alone.

"I hope you don't mind if we stay and have dinner. I've heard a lot of good things about you from your mother and it would give us a chance to get to know one another."

Luke was certain if her smile grew any wider, her head would split in half. He was raised to be a gentleman and knew it wasn't Valerie's fault, so he decided to make the best of it.

Jordan had called in an order to one of her favorite restaurants. She and Andy hadn't felt like going out. They'd rented a couple of movies and planned to just veg on the couch tonight. While the hostess went to get her food, Jordan scanned the restaurant. She blinked and squinted at a couple in the middle of the room. *It couldn't be him*, she thought, so she looked again to make sure. Her shock quickly turned to disbelief and contempt when she realized that, indeed it was true. Luke was having a cozy dinner with a woman Jordan had never seen before. *What a snake*! He'd just put his lovely wife on a plane two days ago. Now here he was out on the town with another woman! *Men like him think they can have their cake and eat it, too. I should go over there and give him a piece of my mind and warn that girl what kind of man she's sitting across from.* Just then, the waitress arrived and handed Jordan a plastic bag filled with white Styrofoam containers. Deciding not to make a scene, she turned and marched out of the restaurant. This is why she'd vowed never to get involved with handsome, sweet-talking men like Luke Kincaid.

Luke and Valerie ordered and talked. She was pleasant enough—but she wasn't Jordan. She laughed a little too much at his attempts at humor and stared at him with flirtatious and hopeful eyes. He had to figure out a way to end the evening without hurting her feelings.

After he paid the check, he walked Valerie to her car. "Thank you for having dinner with me," he said. "But I need to get up early in the morning, so I should be going. I have several jobs coming up that will keep me very busy for the next few months." He shook her hand goodbye before she could suggest they exchange phone numbers or make plans to get together again.

Valerie didn't say anything. She just stood there looking a little stunned as he walked away—like a deer caught in the headlights of an oncoming car.

He was going to pay his mother a visit tomorrow. She had to stay out of his love life. Luke knew she meant well, but it wasn't fair to the unsuspecting females that were tricked into thinking he was available and looking. He wasn't—well not exactly anyway.

The more Luke worked on the old house, the more he thought about Jordan. He wondered if she'd like the paint colors he'd picked or the way he'd remodeled the rooms. Maybe she would have the opportunity to see it one of these days after he sold it to someone new.

The girl from the journal drifted through his mind, too, especially when he went to work on the second floor. Luke could tell by the layout that he was now in the bedroom that must have been M.J.'s.

He found the vent where she used to hide her journal from her pesky, little brother. Just above the white wainscoting, old, peeling wallpaper with vertical stripes of delicate flowers in pinks and yellows covered all four walls. Luke could picture her growing up here, dreaming about Brad here. He could almost feel her presence in the room with him while he painted the walls and refinished the wood floor.

That night when Luke flipped to the next

page in M.J.'s journal, a folded piece of paper fell out.

> *My darling, M.J.,*
>
> *I want to apologize again for my behavior toward you at the hospital and since my return home. I tried to be the man you wanted me to be, but it has become painfully apparent that I cannot. I'm not the same man I was before I left. Someday I hope you can find it in your heart to forgive me. By the time you read this, I'll be gone. Please don't try to find me and do not wait for me. I will not be returning.*
>
> *Please move on with your life, and I do pray that you will find happiness with a man who can truly love you.*
>
> *Brad*

He left her? What a jerk! Luke turned his attention back to the journal.

> *My heart is broken beyond com-prehension. I knew things had been different between us, but I never imag-ined the man I loved would abandon me. Mother found this note leaning*

against the front door and she handed it to me when I came down for breakfast. How could he just leave? Did my love mean nothing to him?

Luke needed to step away from the young woman's story for a while, but that didn't stop him from thinking about her. He found himself wondering about what happened to this mysterious stranger. It felt odd to admit he was developing feelings for her, a woman he'd never met, and one, in all likelihood, he never would.

Caring for two women at one time—M.J. and Jordan— how was that possible? That kind of thing only happened in soap operas and cheap romance novels. But his heart assured him otherwise.

He was falling in love with two women.

One in the past and one in the present.

Chapter 7

Luke showed up at Jordan's house at eight o'clock Saturday morning and let himself in her backyard gate. Odie immediately started barking, alerting the neighborhood that there was an intruder afoot. But as soon as the dog saw that it was Luke, he ran toward him, tongue hanging out and tail wagging.

They'd become friends over the last few weekends, which seem to bother Jordan for some reason. Maybe she took Odie's acceptance of him as some kind of betrayal, a consorting with the enemy.

He set his toolbox down on the grass near the almost finished shed. Glancing up at the house, he caught Jordan peeking out of the kitchen window at him. He waved, but the only response he received was a scowl as she closed the blinds, ignoring his presence. Luke had been working for a couple of hours before he heard the sound of the back door. Jordan emerged from the house wearing cut-offs and an old rock band T-shirt. Today, her ponytail was pulled through the opening in the back of a worn ball cap. She looked like the girl next-door—but sexy. "Morning," Luke said, flashing her a big smile.

"Are you always so cheery this early?" Jordan grumbled

"Most of the time." Shrugging, Luke glanced at his watch. "Besides, it's after ten. Most of the morning is already gone." He noticed the expression lines on her forehead deepen, conveying that she did not share the same appreciation for getting an early start on the day.

"I came out to see if you'd like something to drink?" Crossing her arms over her chest, she added, "I have coffee, soda, or water."

"Water will be fine."

Luke figured that even though it was no secret she didn't want him there, she still felt obligated to show a little hospitality. He wished he knew why she was so unfriendly around him. He hammered a few more nails into the wooden frame before she reappeared. After wiping his hands on the rag he pulled from his back pocket, he reached for the glass of ice water. When his fingers brushed Jordan's, his pulse quickened. His eyes sought hers wondering if he was the only one who had sensed a spark pass between them. The look on her face confirmed he wasn't.

Jordan felt the electricity from their innocent contact and hated the effect he had on her. She didn't want to feel anything for him, but every time they were near each other, every cell in her body reacted. She just had to keep reminding herself that he was unavailable and nothing could ever develop between them. Not that she'd wasted her time thinking about such things. Well—not much anyway.

He finished the water and handed her the glass. "Thank you, Jordan. It's starting to get warm out here and that hit the spot."

Jordan also felt the heat, but it had nothing to do with the numbers on the thermometer.

"No problem," was all she said before turning around and going back into the house.

Once inside, Jordan leaned her back against the cool, wooden surface of the door wondering how she was ever going to get through the rest of the weekends that Luke had to be at her house. Taking a moment to pull herself together, she started on her list of chores, stopping every so often to glance outside at the handsome man in her yard.

The flapping sound of the plastic doggie door alerted Jordan that Odie had returned from one of his neighborhood adventures. Normally he was confined to the safety of the fenced backyard. But sometimes on the weekend when she was home, she would let him run around the cul-de-sac for an hour or so. She'd leave the side gate open allowing him to come and go as he pleased. The little dog never wandered very far. Usually he'd just visit the older couple two houses down, knowing they would have a treat waiting for him.

As she entered the kitchen, a horrible smell greeted her. "Oh my gosh, Odie. What did you roll in now?" The terrier mix stood there in the middle of the floor, staring up at her, and wondering why she was holding her nose and twisting her face like that. "Outside. Now!" she ordered.

Reluctantly, the little dog obeyed, not quite sure what the fuss was all about. After finding the air freshener, Jordan gave the kitchen a good spray and then went to find the dog shampoo. Odie was going to get a bath.

Luke returned from the hardware store just as Jordan finished filling an old metal washtub that sat on the grass not far from the back door. "What's this?"

"Odie must have gotten into a trash can or rolled in something dead. I'm not sure, but he stinks."

The dog tilted his head giving Luke a "who me?" expression with his eyes. "Have fun." He chuckled on his way back toward the shed.

"Gee, thanks."

"Let me know if you need any help holding him down."

Jordan glared at him over her left shoulder. "I think I can handle it."

As the afternoon temperature rose, it wasn't long before Luke worked up more of a sweat with each board he added to the shed. Using his forearm, he wiped the perspiration from his face. Trails of sweat trickled down his spine and stomach. His gray T-shirt grew dark and was soon soaked from the neckline to the bottom hem. Removing it, he hung it over a nearby tree limb to dry.

Jordan peeked up through her lashes and felt her heart race at the sight of his bare chest. His skin was a golden tan and his rippling muscles glistened in the sun.

Out of the corner of his eye, Luke caught

her looking at him. He hadn't removed his shirt to get a reaction from her, yet he had to grin at the way she was trying so hard to hide the fact she was stealing glances at his body.

Thankfully, Odie didn't really mind baths, but keeping still was not something he understood. He played in the water, causing some to overflow the edges of the metal tub, soaking the ground. Jordan had just finished rinsing the squirming bundle of wet fur. When she turned to reach for a towel, Odie's body tensed, followed by a low growl. Jordan turned her head to see what had riled him and instantly knew what was about to happen.

"Odie! No!"

Her attempt to distract him proved unsuccessful. His archenemy, Barney, the gray tabby cat from across the street, was walking across the top of the wooden fence that surrounded the yard. The wet dog flew out of the metal tub, barking fiercely as he bolted toward the unwelcome trespasser.

Luke turned his head to see what all the commotion was about. At the exact same time, Jordan let out a squeal, her arms flailing in the air. Apparently, she'd tried to go after the dog, but her feet slipped on the damp ground. The next second, she fell backwards into the metal tub of stinky, dirty water with a splash.

Rushing to help her, Luke lifted Jordan out with ease, cradling her in his arms. Just as he was about to ask her if she was hurt, he lost his footing and they tumbled down onto the wet grass.

Jordan landed on top of him, still wrapped in his arms, her palms flat on his muscular chest. Their eyes locked just inches apart. "Are you all right?" his voice was low and tender.

All she could do was nod. The flicker of desire in his eyes and the feel of his smooth, warm skin under her fingers took away any ability she had to speak.

"You're very beautiful, Jordan," he whispered. "Your eyes are such a striking shade of blue. I've never seen any like them before."

Her soft curves molded so perfectly against him, it was as if she belonged there. Even though he knew it was a bad idea the moment it popped into his head—and Jordan had given him no reason to think she'd even consider it—he couldn't stop himself. He needed to kiss her. Gently easing her face closer, he pressed his lips to hers and the rest of the world just faded away.

It amazed Jordan how natural it felt and before she realized it, she was kissing him back as if they'd done it a million times before. Her body came alive with emotions and sensations that felt so good, so right. A faint moan escaped her throat as their kissing intensified.

Jordan's unexpected shift in behavior surprised him and his body reacted to her softness and to her eager kisses. Neither of them was aware how long they stayed on the wet grass.

The sound of Odie's barking suddenly broke through the haze that had consumed Jordan the minute Luke started kissing her. She pushed herself away from him, a mixture of panic and anger surging through her. "We shouldn't have done that. How could you do this to me? To her? I need you to leave!" Crying, she scrambled to her feet and dashed toward the house.

"Jordan! What's wrong? Who are you talking about?" Luke rose up on one elbow and called after her, confused by her sudden change in attitude once again.

"Please, Luke, just leave," she shouted over her shoulder as she ran inside the house, slamming the back door.

Trembling, she collapsed into the nearest kitchen chair, letting her head rest against her arms that lay folded on the table. Tears continued to fall as the guilt and shame of what she'd done gripped her heart. The face of the auburn-haired woman she'd delivered flowers to that day entered her mind. Jordan couldn't believe she'd allowed Luke to kiss her like that. And she'd kissed him back. Furious for not being able to resist him, she told herself that she was no different than the woman who had run off with her father, destroying her family all those years ago.

Luke got to his feet and knocked on the back door. "Jordan? I'm sorry if I did anything to upset you. Please, open the door." Her crying was the only sound he could hear and it tugged at his heart. "Jordan, please. Talk to me."

Raising her head slightly, she yelled in the direction of the door, "Go away, Luke. I can't understand how you could do this to Anna! To me!" Jordan's shame and anger propelled her out of the chair. "Now pack up your tools and get off my property!" Then, she turned and ran down the hall to her bedroom.

Luke heard the muffled sound of a door slamming shut. He didn't have a clue as to why Jordan was so mad. She obviously took offense to him kissing her, but what did that have to do with his mother? Whatever the reason, he was done trying to figure it out. Ms. Jordan Shaw definitely had a problem with him. But no matter how much he liked her, he wasn't going to waste time beating his head against a wall any longer.

While he gathered up his tools, he felt eyes staring at him. Looking from window to window, he hoped to see Jordan's face, but she wasn't there. A small whine came from the other direction and Luke turned to find Odie sitting in the grass next to him. The dog's sad eyes looked at him, then at the house.

"I don't know what happened? I don't know what's wrong with her?" Luke released a heavy sigh. "Females...I just don't...I... Which planet did that book say they were from again?" Reaching down, he ruffled the fur on Odie's head, before walking through the backyard gate to his truck.

Later that night, Luke thought about the afternoon at Jordan's and the kiss they'd shared. He probably should regret it, but he didn't. He raked his fingers through his hair, still damp from his shower. He was attracted to her. But as much as he wanted to get to know her better, he realized it wasn't going to happen. He was too busy with his business and the old house to have a relationship any-way—at least that was the excuse he used to help soften the blow to his male ego. Besides, fickle females were too much work.

A few days later, Luke read the next two entries in M.J.'s journal.

> *Just when I'm starting to put my life back together from Brad's disap-pearance, my life has been shattered once again! How could this have hap-pened? The police came to the house yesterday and said Daddy stole a lot of money from the bank. They also found out he purchased plane tickets for him-self and his secretary and they have apparently run off together. What made him do something like this? Mother is beside herself with grief and humiliation from his ultimate betrayal.*

Mother can't bear the stares and whispers that have already started from the people in town. She's making plans to leave and go back East to live with her sister, Linda. A.J. will be going with her and will start high school there in the fall. I'll be going too, at least for the summer, then I'll be off to college. Mother doesn't want to leave the home she grew up in. But her father has passed away and Grams can't take care of it all by herself. With Daddy on the run from the law, she has no reason to stay. She'll hire someone to take care of the place and then maybe someday we can all return and start over. There are a lot of memories in this house, but I'm going to remember only the good ones. All the laughter, the parties, the fun. And, of course, Grams. Maybe one day this house will again be filled with happiness and joy, and bring our family together. I'm off to start a new chapter in my life. I'm excited and nervous at the same time, but Grams said, "Being afraid to experience life is like brushing your teeth before you eat. It just don't make any sense. Being nervous is your body's way of preparing you for a new adventure." I made a decision and talked to Mother about it this afternoon. I'm going to legally change my name. I'll use my middle name and change my last name to Gram's maiden name. I don't want anyone to know that I'm related to Stewart Price. The shame Daddy has brought on this family is unforgivable.

This young girl had really been through a lot, and Luke felt sorry for her. Now days, most people didn't make that big a fuss over infidelity, at least not quite so much as they did back then. But Luke wasn't most people. He couldn't comprehend what kind of man could say those wedding vows, father two children, and then just abandon his family like that. If this guy didn't love his wife anymore, he should have gotten a divorce before hooking up with someone else. No wonder M.J. wanted to change her name.

He hadn't seen or spoken to Jordan since that day in her back yard, but that didn't stop him from thinking about her—and remembering that kiss. It had only taken him two more

Saturdays to finish the shed, and now that it was done he was anxious to get back to work on the old house.

One afternoon, while remodeling the kitchen, he was busy taking measurements for new shelving in the large walk-in pantry when he noticed some writing on the inside door frame.

He took out his flashlight so he could get a better look. Horizontal marks, some more faint than others, went up the piece of wood. There were letters next to the lines, some were an "M" and some were an "A." It took a minute for him to realize it was a growth chart, like the one at his grandparent's house.

He pried the narrow strip of wood from the frame, but when he went outside to toss it on the pile of stuff to haul away, he felt a strange tingling in his hand. He frowned at the old markings. *This is crazy, there's nothing special about this board. The kids that once leaned against it are long gone.* He threw it onto the heap of other junk and went back inside. As he continued to work over the next couple of hours, those initials from the pantry nagged at his heart. Before he left for the day, he retrieved from the trash pile the slender board that had tormented him and placed it just inside the back door. Instantly, a wave of calm washed over him. "I must be coming down with the flu. My body's behaving very strangely."

Chapter 8

The dirt parking lot of the fairgrounds was more crowded than Luke had anticipated. He'd made plans to take his mom out to lunch today, but when he picked her up, she asked if they could stop by the artist festival first. He hesitated, but finally agreed. He had no real interest in any of the items on display—there were quilts, paintings, sculptures—but these things made his mom happy. After entering the large metal building, Anna went one way, promising not to be long. Luke strolled over to the section where the photographs hung on display. There were several categories; portraits, action, scenery, color, and black and white. Large ribbons indicating Best in Show, First, and Second place had already been awarded.

Jordan had been looking forward to this day for months. If she won today, it would certainly be a tremendous boost for the reputation of her shop. "It looks awesome, boss,"

Darcy gushed, snapping her gum. "You're gonna win, I just know it."

"Thanks, I hope so."

Jordan's stomach felt a little queasy as she glanced down at her watch for the third time in the last twenty minutes. The judging was to start at one o'clock and it was only a few minutes past noon. Chewing on her fingernail, she paced back and forth second-guessing herself. All the nagging doubts and "what ifs" started, one by one, creeping into her brain. *I shouldn't have put the red one and the orange one so close to each other. Maybe I should've used a bigger vase. Is that yellow rose wilting?* She closed her eyes and sighed. *What's done is done. I can't change it.* All she could do now was wait.

Thinking a breath of fresh air and a change of surroundings would help her nerves, she headed toward the front of the building. She was almost to the door when she turned her head to take another glance back at her arrangement. Completely lost in thought, she suddenly collided with someone.

Startled and embarrassed, she began to apologize as strong hands reached out to steady her. When she looked up, there stood Luke Kincaid. He certainly appeared at the most inconvenient times. The spark in his dark eyes and the dazzling smile that she'd grown accustomed to seeing on his handsome face was absent. Jordan's thoughts traveled again to that day in her backyard and her cheeks flushed at the memory of the kiss they'd shared. But those flutters of pleasure were soon replaced by anger. "Well, if it isn't 'Bob the Builder.' You seem to have a habit of showing up unexpectedly, buzzing around like a pesky little gnat. What are you doing here? I know, I bet you're here to sign up for some knitting classes or the seminar on the best time to plant petunias, am I right?"

Other than a slight twitch at one corner of his mouth at her taunting, Luke's steely expression remained intact. His presence seemed to fluster her and on some level that pleased him. Her attitude toward him had obviously not changed since the last time he'd seen her.

"Ms. Shaw, you really should be more careful."

His hands still lingered on her arms. And even though Jordan had made it perfectly clear that she wasn't interested in him, he had to fight down the urge to pull her to him and kiss her again.

She shrugged out of his grasp. "Excuse me?"

"You should watch where you're going," he stated bluntly.

An icy stare was her only response, before she smoothed her clothes back into place.

"How's the shed working out?" Luke asked, attempting to make small talk with the woman who turned him inside out every time he was near her.

"Fine."

"If you have any problems with it, just give my office a call."

"I'm sure if you're half as good as you think you are, that won't be necessary."

Her sarcastic remark irritated him, causing the muscles along his jaw to tighten. If she didn't like him, fine, but he didn't appreciate her insulting the quality of his work.

Their eyes remained locked on each other, both searching for a sign that the other was going to be the first to end this standoff. A slight five o'clock shadow enhanced his rugged good looks. Unfortunately for her, Jordan's stubborn streak was no match for her female hormones. *Of all the people I could have run into today, why did it have to be him?*

Her voice softened slightly. "I'm sorry for bumping into you." She saw the muscles in Luke's face relax. She noticed his gaze was focused on her lips, no doubt recalling that same kiss she couldn't wipe from her thoughts. A hint of color appeared on her cheeks.

"I heard you'd submitted an entry and I was on my way over to wish you good luck. Is it the tall one in the crystal vase?"

She nodded in response.

"Your arrangement is spectacular."

"Thank you."

"You look beautiful, Jordan."

Luke's dimpled smile brought to life the sensations she'd experienced every time she saw him. Suddenly, she felt lightheaded under his appraising stare, hating that he always had such an effect on her. Why did *this* particular man, the one she needed to avoid the most, always manage to make her feel like she was the only woman in the room? She swallowed hard to push down her emotions and repeated her earlier question. "What are you doing here?"

"I'm here with Anna."

The color drained from Jordan's face.

"Anna! Anna's *here*?" Her eyes nervously

scanned the crowd for the woman who'd met her at the door that day.

"Yeah, we were on our way to lunch and—"

"What?" Jordan scowled at him, "You're standing here smiling at me like that and *she's* here!"

"What does Anna being here have to do with how I look at you?" Luke didn't understand why every time he saw Jordan, she kept bringing up the subject of his mother.

"I can't believe you're such a jerk. Why do handsome men seem to think that they can act like this? I'm sure your wife—"

Luke held up his hands to stop her. "Whoa, wait a second. Wife?" Both curious and confused by her remark, he felt his eyebrows draw together. "What are you talking about, Jordan?"

"You know, *Anna*?" she said, waving her arms around out of frustration. "The woman you ordered that large bouquet of flowers for. The one with auburn hair and large diamond wedding ring."

Jordan wiggled her left ring finger in his face.

Luke stared at her for a moment before it all became clear. "So you think..." A hearty rumble came from deep in his chest. "That explains a lot."

Anger flared in Jordan's eyes. "This isn't funny! You should be ashamed of yourself! First, you flirt with me while you're ordering flowers for Anna, then you dance with that blonde *and* me at the bar. I even saw you having dinner with yet *another* woman two days after you put Anna on a plane. And now, here you are, flirting with me *again*, all the while married to that beautiful woman."

He struggled to hold in another burst of laughter. "Wait here, Jordan. Please? I'll be right back."

A few minutes later, Luke returned with a lovely, older woman. "Jordan," he said with a twinkle in his eye. "I'd like you to meet Anna Kincaid—my mother."

"Your mother?" Stunned, Jordan looked from Luke's face to the woman's. She pointed with her index finger. "You're—Anna?"

"Yes. Luke told me that you're the young lady who created that stunning arrangement for my birthday. It was gorgeous! Thank you so much."

Luke just stood there smiling like the Cheshire Cat.

After all this time, he'd finally solved the

mystery behind Jordan's nasty attitude toward him.

"But then who was..." Jordan looked at Luke. "When I came to the door, a very attractive woman signed for the flowers."

"That was my sister-in-law, Audra. She's married to my brother, Philip, and she was visiting my mother while he was out of town on business."

"Sister-in-law?"

Anna looked to Luke for an explanation.

"Jordan thought Audra was *my* wife and that the flowers were for her."

"Oh, my. I'm sorry about the misunderstanding."

"It gets worse," he continued. "Jordan saw me at the bar a few weeks ago talking and dancing with Carl's daughter, Amy. She thought I was a cad and out on the town carousing like a cheating gigolo. She saw me having dinner with Valerie that night at the steakhouse, too."

"I could see how that might look if you didn't know Luke," Anna commented.

Heat and color flooded Jordan's cheeks, turning them as red as the roses in her display just a few feet away. Silence filled the air for several long seconds before anyone spoke.

"Do you have an entry in the floral competition?" Anna asked, changing the subject.

"Yes, that one over there," Jordan answered shyly, pointing in the direction of her flowers.

"It's wonderful and very unique. You're extremely talented, Ms. Shaw. I'm sure the judges will reward your creativity." Anna turned to her son. "Luke, I'll only be a moment longer, do you mind?"

"Of course not. I'll meet you by the front door whenever you're ready."

Anna gave him a loving squeeze on the arm before turning to Jordan. "It was nice to meet you, Ms. Shaw."

"You too, Mrs. Kincaid."

After his mother walked away, Luke looked at Jordan, "Now that we have that all cleared up, maybe we can start over."

She gazed into his face, "All right, but I'm so embarrassed by all those things I said to you."

Flashing a sexy smile in her direction, he leaned down close to her left ear. "I know just how you can make it up to me."

"Oh?" Jordan replied, thinking maybe her first instincts about him being a playboy were really true.

A flicker of mischief appeared on his chiseled face, like that of a two-year-old little boy when he's up to something. "Have dinner with me Friday night."

Jordan was happier than she wanted to admit at the discovery that he wasn't married. "I'd like that." She paused a moment. "Can I ask you a question?"

"Sure," he replied.

"Why do you call your mother by her first name?"

Luke chuckled. "It started out as an act of teen-age rebellion. After a while it just became habit. She puts up with it even though I'm sure she'd rather I just use 'Mom.' So, I'll give you a call at work the first part of the week."

A new wave of shivers trickled down her spine. "Okay."

"Bye, Jordan. And good luck."

"Thanks."

She felt excited as she watched him walk away, like a schoolgirl with a crush on the star quarterback who had just asked her to the prom. Memories of their previous encounters came to mind: the dance, the kiss, and how she'd fought down all the feelings they'd stirred up within her. But right now, she needed to focus. In a few minutes the judges would be announcing the winners and she couldn't stand up there with a goofy grin on her face.

Wandering back to her display, she awaited her fate. The judges awarded her second place. Jordan felt a small twinge of disappointment, but was overall very excited. This was her first time entering the statewide contest and she was proud of her arrangement. She received a small monetary prize that she could definitely use, but the most important thing to her was the exposure for her shop.

Monday morning, Jordan was busy doing paperwork in her office when Darcy came in. "Hey, boss. Are you okay? You were totally robbed on Saturday. You so should've won. I wonder if one of those old blue-hairs bribed the judges." Her voice held the sincerity of youthful indignation.

"Thanks, Darcy, but I'm fine."

Jordan appreciated her employee's concern, but had to swallow a chuckle at her dramatic explanation of the event. They discussed the schedule for this week, and then Darcy left to make some deliveries.

Luke had read in the Sunday paper about Jordan coming in second, and he felt like doing something to let her know he was thinking about her. He wanted to congratulate her, but buying her flowers wasn't the answer, for obviously reasons, and a box of chocolates seemed kind of corny. After racking his brain, he came up with the perfect idea.

About three o'clock Monday afternoon, the bell chimed above the front door of Jordan's shop. "I'll be right with you," she called. She rounded the corner and there stood Luke, with a bunch of wildflowers clutched in one hand and a card in the other.

"I'm sorry you didn't win first place. The judges must have been blind."

Jordan stifled a laugh at the sight of this rugged man standing in front of her with puppy dog eyes and a few drooping blossoms attempting to make her feel better. "There's always next year. Are those for me?" she asked, pointing at the unique bouquet.

"Ah, yeah. I didn't know what to get you and since you like flowers, I thought maybe you'd like these."

His boyish smile and thoughtfulness warmed her heart. "That was very sweet of you, Mr. Kincaid." With a sparkle in her eyes, she motioned for him to follow her. "Come in the back while I find a vase."

Luke and Jordan talked awhile, then she showed him around the shop.

It was comfortable and nice being in her company. He was relieved she liked his gift. Inside the card were two tickets to the movies for this weekend.

After Luke left, Jordan gently fingered the delicate petals of the yellow and purple wild-flowers sitting on her desk. *Handsome, sexy, and sweet. Mr. Luke Kincaid, you seem too good to be true.* She knew she should still keep her guard up around him, just in case. She didn't want to jump into anything, unsure if she could *really* trust him quite yet.

But, Jordan knew it was too late. Her heart had already fallen for him.

Chapter 9

Over the next couple of weeks, Luke and Jordan went to the movies and out to dinner. She found out that he hated broccoli, and he found out that her favorite flavor of ice cream was strawberry.

The two were having dinner at Juanita's on Wednesday night when Luke looked up at Jordan. "Do you like county fairs?"

Her face lit up. "Who doesn't? They make me feel like a kid again. Why?"

"Hilldale's is this weekend. Would you like to go?"

"I'd love to."

Luke smiled at her childlike excitement. "I suppose you're going to want me to go on those crazy rides, too," he grumbled, rolling his eyes.

"Of course. Why? Is a big, tough guy like you afraid of a few spins and flips?"

"I'll have you know," he boasted, "I'm the all-time record holder for the most trips on

The Zipper in one night." He arched his brows with male satisfaction.

"Really? Impressive. How old were you?"

"Wh—what?" he stammered slightly.

"How old were you?" she repeated, knowing she'd caught him bragging a little too much.

He fidgeted in his chair, clearing his throat before he answered. "Well...I...ah, I was ten. But, that doesn't matter. I'm still the record holder for the entire fifth grade at Watson Elementary." He tried to convince Jordan that it was still an important achievement. But when he gazed into her dancing aqua eyes, his attempt to keep a straight face failed and he released a hearty chuckle.

"Don't worry, hot shot, your secret's safe with me," she assured him as her laughter blended with his.

It was early Saturday evening when Luke arrived to pick Jordan up for their date to the fair. She walked out of her house wearing a summery top and denim capris. Her light brown hair had been released from the usual ponytail and its silky strands glistened in the fading sunlight. The vision before him caused his testosterone to go on full alert. Meeting her at the bottom of the porch steps, he scanned her up and down. "You look too good to take to the fair. Maybe we should go back inside, order a pizza and hang out on the couch." He wiggled his eyebrows at her.

Jordan blushed at the devilish gleam in his eyes, but she loved the way his words made her feel desired. Shaking her finger at him, she replied, "You behave yourself, Mr. Kincaid. *We* are going to the fair."

Luke wrapped his arms around her, inhaling the sweet smell of her perfume, "Oh, all right, if you insist."

On their way to the fair, she slid over next to him, giving him a quick peck on the cheek. Her reward was one of his sexy smiles, which always produced a fluttering sensation in her stomach.

The sounds of laughter and ear-piercing cries could be heard from the parking lot of the fairgrounds. Some were shrieks of delight and some were screams of terror. As they grew closer, the air was filled with a mixture of smells; dust stirred up by the children running excitedly to the next ride, foods ranging from barbeque to funnel cakes and, of course, manure.

After walking through the turnstile, Luke turned to Jordan. "Okay, where to first?"

She scanned the map they were given at the entrance and looked at the schedule of events before answering him. "Um, let's start with the petting zoo."

He motioned with his hand. "Lead the way."

Once inside the metal holding pen, a small herd of bloated-looking pygmy goats immediately surrounded them begging for the food pellets that fair-goers could purchase at the entrance. A gray and black goat started staring at Luke the minute he walked in and tracked the man's every move.

"Aren't the baby ones adorable," Jordan cooed as she and Luke squatted down to pet them.

Just as she said that, the animal that had been stalking Luke came up and nudged his leg. When he didn't immediately offer it a snack, the goat head-butted him in the side, tipping him over onto the straw-covered ground. The horned animal stood there just glaring down at him with black, sideways pupils, like a victor savoring the defeat of its opponent. A few seconds later, the goat turned and waddled away in search of his next target. A loud snicker escaped Jordan's mouth.

"Yeah, just adorable," he grumbled, then stood and brushed off his jeans.

Once the fat little moochers finished off all Luke and Jordan had to offer, the animals moved on to their next victim. Lingering a while longer, the two of them went from pen to pen, each one containing the standard farm animals. Cute baby piglets squealed and ran for the safety of their mother when a toddler charged up to their enclosure. A timid little calf peeked under the large belly of its mother, not sure what to make of all the sounds and smells in the air.

Next, they went into the rabbit barn where Jordan ignored the "Do Not Touch" signs and poked her index finger through the wire mesh of each cage to stroke their plush fur. "I had a rabbit once. My mom bought it for me after the fair one year when I was six years old. He was so cute and I named him Leo. He had droopy ears and was tri-colored, like a calico cat. He wasn't very friendly though, he bit me every time I tried to hold him. And then one day when I came home from school, my mom told me he had died." Sadness washed through Jordan. "We buried him in the back yard."

Luke gave her a sympathetic nod and,

with a comforting touch, rubbed her back, but he didn't say anything. Words weren't necessary. They made their way around to the rest of the livestock on display, the pungent smell of manure assaulting their noses. Especially awful was the stench of the pigpens.

Hand in hand, they drifted up and down the rows where carnies beckoned kids to try out the games. They also taunted the men, especially if they were with a woman, challenging them to impress the lady by winning her a teddy bear.

Jordan motioned with her head in the direction of the colorful booths. "Do you ever play?"

"No, I don't need a fish or a mirrored beer sign, and I'm definitely not going to pay ten dollars for a cheap, fifty cent stuffed toy."

At the end of the last row stood a little photo kiosk. "Come on, let's get our picture taken." Tugging at Luke's arm, she coaxed him in the direction of the phone-booth sized box.

"Why not?" He shrugged and sat down on the small stool and, after Jordan took a seat on his lap, he pulled the red curtain shut. "You ready?"

"Let's do it!"

He inserted the coins in the slot and with each flash, they took one silly pose after another. A couple frames of funny, twisted up faces; another giving each other rabbit ears with their fingers; and in the final picture, they kissed. While waiting outside for the photo strip to be dispensed, Luke and Jordan laughed and hugged each other with playful excitement.

"Being here reminds me of when I was a little girl. My parents brought Andy and me to the fair every year. We had so much fun." After reviewing the different poses and making fun of themselves, they put their arms around each other and strolled in the direction of the food vendors.

"What are you hungry for?" Luke asked.

"Corn dog, of course. You have to have one when you come to the county fair. Didn't you know that?" she challenged with a hint of amusement in her voice.

"I guess I missed that requirement when I was going through the rule book on county fair etiquette," he teased.

"And then, before we leave, we have to buy some cotton candy."

"No thanks."

"Excuse me? No cotton candy at the fair?"

She shook her head in disbelief with a gleam in her eyes. "That's just un-American."

They both chuckled again. Luke loved to hear her laugh and wanted to believe that he was partly responsible for her happiness that day.

They wandered through the buildings that displayed the paintings submitted by local artists and each voted for their favorites. As evening approached, the vibrantly colored lights on the midway flashed to the music, illuminating everything in the area. Sounds of bells and whistles from the games and rides intensified in the night air as they blended with the roar of metal wheels flying across steel tracks.

Most of the smaller kids had now gone home with their exhausted parents leaving only the teenagers to cruise the fair in small packs. Giggling girls who wore too much make-up, skin-tight jeans, or miniskirts, paraded in their three-inch spiky heels leaving tiny holes in the dirt. Boys in tank tops and T-shirts, with the latest cool logos, and caps worn backwards swaggered along not far behind. With hormones raging, each gender strutted for the other, performing the flirtatious dance of adolescence.

Luke and Jordan smiled at different ones, recalling vividly the memories from their own past, when they too, played the time-honored game. It was like the first step to freedom, a rite of passage. Finally, you were allowed to go to the fair at night without the watchful eyes of your meddlesome parents ruining all your fun.

"How about a spin on the Ferris Wheel?" Luke pointed up at the red and yellow chaser lights outlining the edges of the giant flashing ride.

Jordan grinned as the colors flickered and danced in Luke's dark eyes. "I'd like that."

With their fingers intertwined, they headed in that direction. Luke gave the tickets to the man standing at the gate. He and Jordan climbed the metal steps, proceeded across the uneven platform, and eased down on one of ride's vacant green bench seats. After they settled in, a seedy-looking carnie pulled the metal safety bar down in front of them and, with a clank, secured it in place.

Luke put his arm around Jordan's shoulder and she snuggled up next to him. She felt happier than she had in a long time.

A quick jolt and the ride began to move. As it approached the top, they could see out over the entire fairgrounds below them. It looked like a tiny city of brightly colored lights. Above them, thousands of stars twinkled in the clear summer night sky.

"I've had a lot of fun today," Jordan said, beaming up at Luke. "Thank you for bringing me here."

"I'm glad, and you're welcome. I had a good time, too," he responded, staring into her beautiful face.

The ride went around a couple of more times and on the third rotation, it stopped suddenly when Luke and Jordan were at the very top. He turned slightly toward her, at least as far as he could, his ability to move hindered by the security bar. The breeze blew strands of hair across Jordan's cheek. Reaching up, he gently tucked them behind her ear, letting his thumb graze her jaw line.

A rush of heat spread through her in response to his tender touch. He leaned over and pressed his lips softly against hers. When he pulled back, his eyes reflected the desire he obviously felt in his heart.

"Jordan," he said, his voice a raspy whisper. "I need to tell you something. I...I'm falling in love with you."

Tears were on the verge of escaping her

eyes as she looked deep into his smoldering brown eyes. "Oh, Luke, I'm falling for you, too."

He placed his palm against her cheek, guiding her face towards his. They kissed again, this time holding nothing back. Neither of them noticed that the ride had started to move again until they heard a grumbling noise. When they looked up, there stood the same shady looking character who'd secured the safety bar scowling down at them. After releasing them, he pointed in the direction of the exit.

Once they left the platform, the two leaned against each other laughing out loud at being caught kissing and the expression on the carnie's face. They were walking away when they overheard a conversation between a pair of teenage girls standing nearby. They'd witnessed what had happened. Jordan guessed them to be about thirteen, and thought to herself how they were trying way too hard to be perceived as older and much more worldly than they really were.

"Oh my gosh! Did you see them? That is so gross!" the taller one in the low cut, red shirt scowled.

"I know! Old people like them shouldn't

do that kinda stuff in public!" her friend in the yellow sundress chimed in.

Their disgust plain on their faces, the girls eyed Luke and Jordan.

He winked at Jordan. "Want to have a little fun?"

At first she was confused, then he leaned over and whispered his plan into her ear. She nodded, agreeing to be his accomplice.

In a voice just loud enough for the obnoxious teens to hear, he announced, "Are you ready to go, sugar pie? I gotta get home and pop one of those magic, little blue pills before we fire up the hot tub and get busy." He wiggled his hips, then for added effect, he gave Jordan's behind a little slap with his hand.

She rested her palms against Luke's chest, responding with a high-pitched giggle, "You got it big daddy."

The eyes of the two adolescent girls flew open and they shrieked with horror before dashing off to tell their friends about the crazy and creepy old couple.

Luke roared with laughter and Jordan slapped at his arm. "You're terrible."

"No question about it. But it was fun seeing the looks on their faces. Sorry about the tap on your backside, but it needed to be done in order for them to get the full effect."

His mischievous smirk told Jordan, he wasn't the least bit sorry—and truthfully, neither was she. "Uh huh, just don't try it again, Mr. Kincaid," she warned him playfully.

He offered her a proper military salute. "Yes, ma'am."

She motioned in the direction the girls had bolted. "Were we ever like that?"

"I'm afraid so," he responded. "Don't you remember the first time you saw your parents kiss after you became a teenager?"

Squishing up her face, Jordan placed her fingertips over her mouth. "Oh, you're right, that *was* awful. Luke glanced towards the girls who had now joined a group of their friends, and by their shocked expressions, were relaying the whole story of what had just happened. The teens pointed in the direction of Luke and Jordan. He waved at them, causing the whole group to take off running again to the opposite side of the fair grounds.

"Stop it, Luke, they're probably going to find a security guard and accuse you of being a dirty old man."

Jiggling his eyebrows, he flashed her a wicked grin. "I am."

A shiver raced up Jordan's spine as her

mind pictured all the things those two little words implied. She shook her head and chuckled. "Come on, Casanova, buy me some cotton candy and let's get out of here."

Comfortable silence surrounded them in the cab of Luke's truck as they drove through the city streets. "You're kind of quiet, is everything all right?"

"Mmm." She scooted across the seat to get closer. "I'm fine, just a little tired. Today was a great day."

The way her soft, feminine body felt nestled up against him just added to his overwhelming desire for her. It had been a long time since Luke had felt this way about a woman. It was going to take all the willpower he could gather to control his need to act on those urges. Jordan was special. He didn't want to mess things up by getting physical with her too soon. Although, he'd already envisioned them making love on several occasions, now was not the time to dwell on any of them.

"Do you want to come in for some coffee?" she offered, her head still resting on his shoulder as he pulled into her driveway.

"You got decaf?"

"Yup, bought some the other day, just for you."

Following her inside, he leaned his hip against the granite countertop, watching her bustle around her kitchen. It was homey and reminded him of how he'd felt when he visited his grandma's house as a kid. After Jordan filled the coffee pot, he reached for her, pulling her to him. She draped her arms around his neck and melted into him as they kissed—this time free of metal bars and prying eyes.

Luke lifted his head, licking his lips, "Um, sweet. Let me try that again."

Jordan smiled, a twinkle in her eye. "I didn't think you liked cotton candy?"

"I don't, but on you, it tastes delicious."

His response was accompanied by a devilish grin.

Jordan's heart skipped a beat at his sexy teasing and soon found herself wrapped in his strong embrace. She buried her fingers deep in Luke's black hair as they released their undeniable passion for each other. The raw and exciting feelings that come from the overpowering passion of a new found love. His kisses were driving her crazy, his musky cologne stirring wonderful tremors deep in her stomach.

Unrestrained moans filled the room fueling the growing desires inside each of them. Luke slipped his hands inside the back of Jordan's shirt, caressing her silky, warm skin. It felt so good to touch her, to hold her. The talk he'd had with himself in the truck about not moving too fast was quickly becoming a distant memory. One hand slid down her side to her narrow waist, triggering a raspy groan from his throat.

The low, manly sound broke through the haze of passion, and Jordan suddenly flinched at his touch. Releasing a shallow gasp, she stepped back, breaking all contact between them. She'd been so consumed by her own desperate and intense need, she hadn't paid attention to the location of his hands.

It took a moment for him to respond, "Jordan?" he asked panting for air. "What's—wrong?" Wide, startled eyes stared back at him. "I'm sorry if I did something—you didn't want me to. I swear I wasn't going to—"

Jordan held up her hand and closed her eyes for a second, still trying to catch her breath. With a slight shake of her head, she tried to focus. "No...I...ah, it's okay. You just caught me off guard—that's all. But, it would probably be a good idea to stop before—well, you know."

The look in Jordan's eyes finished her thought.

"Of course. I don't want us to do anything unless you're ready. Trust me, I'm not that kind of guy," he assured her. Awkward silence hung between them for several seconds before he spoke again. "I guess I should be getting home." He gave her a tentative grin then headed for the door.

"Wait." Jordan caught up to him just as he reached for the doorknob. "I think we should talk about what just happened. I need to explain—"

"It's fine, really. Things got a little carried away and—"

"Luke, please, just hear me out," Jordan pleaded, placing her hand on his arm.

Searching her face and seeing the vulnerability in her eyes, he couldn't say no.

They sat down on the couch and she exhaled a long sigh before gazing into his face. "I don't want you to think I didn't enjoy being in your arms and kissing you, because I did, very much. And to be honest, I've thought about being with you." A hint of color and heat filled her cheeks. "It's just that—"

"You really don't have to do this."

"I need you to know why I had to break up our little hormone party." She released a nervous laugh, hoping to lighten the mood. "I meant what I said tonight, I am falling for you." She swallowed, taking a moment to gather her courage. "I don't want to make love with anyone until I'm married." She stared at him, curious to see his reaction to her announcement.

Luke studied her face, "Are you...a..."

Jordan knew what he was going to ask, "No, I'm not a virgin. I made this decision because I've had a couple of bad experiences in the past where I was led to believe that a man loved me, but after sleeping together, he decided I wasn't what he was looking for."

Luke knew all too well the kind of guy she was talking about. Unfortunately, when he was young and stupid, he'd behaved like that toward a girl who'd deserved better. The expression on Jordan's face was so sweet and sincere. He reached for her hand and gently wove his fingers through hers. "I'm sorry you were treated like that. Is that why you were so standoffish to me when we first met? You thought I was only out for a one-night stand?"

"Yeah, I'm pretty sure it was. You see,

you remind me a little of my college boy-friend—" Jordan stopped, not sure how much of her past to share with him, everything was still so new. Lowering her head as if she were shy or embarrassed, she continued. "Oh, it doesn't matter, I was just rambling."

Luke placed his index finger under Jordan's chin, lifting her face so he could see into her eyes. "I'd love to hear about your life, unless you don't feel comfortable sharing the stories with me." His voice was caring as he tucked a strand of silky hair behind her ear, just like on the Farris Wheel.

His strong calloused hand touched her skin with such gentleness. She looked deep into his tender, brown eyes, while her mind wrestled with her heart. "Well, I suppose it would help you to understand why I acted so awful to you." Jordan gathered her thoughts and took a deep breath. "His name was Greg. I met him half way through my freshman year at Fairfield College. He was a junior and dev-astatingly handsome. All the girls went out of their way to flirt with him, and he enjoyed the attention. I was shy and not that experienced in the area of men and relationships." She blushed after admitting how naïve she'd been. "For some reason, Greg decided to set his sights on me. I was flattered and nervous at the same time. He said all the right things and did all the right things, and before long, I fell head over heels in love with him.

"One evening at his apartment off campus, he talked about how much he wanted to marry me. I was so happy. We made love for the first time that night." She paused for a moment as the memories of his touch and his cologne rushed into her senses. She fought to hold back the tears.

"There were only a few weeks left of school and with finals, we didn't see each other as much as I wanted. The day he left to go back home for the summer, I sobbed my eyes out. He tried to comfort me by promising that he'd call and make plans to come visit me. Things were difficult, but he kept in touch for a while. I was working at a flower shop in Fairfield and was thankful I had a job, which kept me busy and helped occupy my time. By the end of July, Greg's calls were coming less and less often, and when I asked him to come see me, he always found an excuse why he couldn't.

"Finally one weekend, I took off and drove to his hometown to surprise him. I stopped at a cafe outside of town to ask for directions. A waitress with bright blue eye shadow and a tall red beehive hairdo asked if I was one of Greg's college friends in town for his wedding. I remember feeling like my world had just caved in around me. I was devastated." Her fragile voice quivered, even after all these years.

Luke reached for Jordan. She was trembling and cold. She gave him a faint smile, conveying a silent thank you. "I found out later that he'd been engaged to this other girl the entire year he was at Fairfield." Her eyes sought his again as she drew in a shaky breath, trying to get control of her emotions before she continued. "I can't tolerate being lied to or deceived, so now do you understand why I—"

Luke interrupted. "Jordan, you don't have to explain any more. I'm so sorry that jackass treated you so badly. I can see now how you thinking Audra was my wife and me flirting with you every chance I got could make me seem like him. I promise you I'll never pressure you into doing anything you don't want to do or aren't ready for."

"Okay." Jordan wanted to believe him—with all of her heart she wanted to believe him—but she still didn't know if she could.

There was such an overpowering physical attraction between them and that could definitely cloud her judgment. Luke Kincaid had an intense effect on her. He stirred up such strong feelings that it scared her. Jordan knew the damage he could do to her heart.

That night as Luke lay in bed, he replayed the story Jordan had told him. But also, on his mind was the memory of her smooth skin under his hands, the passionate kisses they shared, and the longing for her that still hadn't left his body. He knew he was going to have a difficult time sleeping. The visions of Jordan wouldn't let him rest. *Yeah, this is going to be a long night,* he thought. Finally, after an hour of tossing and turning, he threw back the covers and stomped to the bathroom in need of a cold shower.

Chapter 10

Jordan invited Luke over for dinner the next weekend. While she stirred pots on the stove, he chopped ingredients for the salad. Odie was in and out of his doggie door, checking every so often to see if anything yummy had accidentally fallen on the kitchen floor.

After gathering a cucumber and a bundle of green onions from the frig, Luke peered over Jordan's shoulder, inhaling the wonderful aromas. "It smells delicious."

"Thanks." Leaning her head back against him, she had to admit how happy Luke made her and how right this felt. The two of them cooking a meal together, relaxed, no pretenses or concerns about impressing the other. She placed a sweet kiss on his cheek before leaning forward to reach for the salt and pepper.

Instead of returning to the table, he set the vegetables down on the kitchen counter and stepped behind Jordan, pressing his body against hers. Wrapping his arms around her waist, Luke squeezed her affectionately, resting his cheek next to her temple. "This is much more fun than going out to eat."

"Why do you say that?"

"Cuz I can flirt with the cook." A low mischievous chuckle escaped his lips. With a slight turn of his head, his warm lips moved lightly, like a whisper, over the soft skin of Jordan's neck.

Vibrations like tiny fingers trickled down her spine, producing an involuntary shiver, affecting every cell in her body. Her reaction to his touch quickly transformed his harmless teasing into overwhelming desire. A small whimper escaped Jordan's mouth as she turned her face toward him. The kissing ignited their passion and longing for each other, powerful and demanding. Jordan lifted her hand, and cupped his jaw, easing his lips closer to hers. After a few precious moments, they separated, breathless, eyes locked on each other. Two hearts pounding wildly.

A drop of boiling water splashed from one of the saucepans, landing on Luke's arm. "I think you're burning our dinner."

Jordan's head was still foggy from the intense feelings he'd stirred up in her. She noticed an impish smirk had replaced the raw lust that'd filled his eyes. "What?"

"The dinner? It's burning."

"Oh, no!"

She pushed Luke away and intently inspected each of the pot and pans in front of her. When she was satisfied that everything was fine, she sent him back across the room to finish the salad. He obeyed like a reprimanded child, but inside he was happier than he'd been in a long time.

After dinner, they plopped themselves down on the couch. "That was an excellent meal, thank you."

"I'm glad you liked it." Jordan beamed then quickly added, "But it was almost ruined, thanks to you."

"Me?"

"Yes, you." Jordan rubbed her neck. "You distracted me." Glancing at each other, they both started to chuckle at the prospect of explaining to the insurance adjuster what led to the fire and smoke damage in her kitchen. "Would you like some dessert?"

"I'd love more of what I tasted earlier." He winked shamelessly.

Jordan blushed. "Funny, real funny." She

slapped at his arm pretending to be irritated with him, but her body betrayed her by trembling at the memory of his kisses.

They drank their coffee in the living room and snacked on homemade oatmeal raisin cookies.

"Did you grow up here in Hilldale?"

Jordan nodded. "Just outside of town." Nostalgia engulfed her as scenes from her childhood flooded her mind. "It was a beautiful old house and I used to love playing outside. There were big trees that bordered the backyard, and their leaves would turn the most vibrant shades of yellows and reds and oranges in the fall. I can still remember the way they crunched under our feet when Andy and I chased each other back and forth during a game of tag. The sound seemed to intensify in the cool autumn air, especially when we wanted to play hide and seek. We would rake the fallen leaves into a pile and take turns jumping in the middle of it—that is if the wind didn't get to them first. Sometimes, if the breeze was just right, it looked like a mini tornado of swirling colors flying up in the air." Jordan laughed as she demonstrated with her hands the scene she'd just described.

"Grams would make us gather them up

and fill a big metal barrel. When we were done, she'd go out and burn them, just a trickle of smoke at first. Then when the driest ones caught, yellow and orange flames would fill the container. The smoke had a pungent smell, spicy and earthy. After the ashes had cooled, she spread them around in her garden, swearing that was why she could grow the best vegetables in three counties. Fall was never complete without that smell."

A gentle sigh revealed to Luke how important these memories were to her.

"In the winter, I loved how the snow would drape on the branches of the pine trees and make everything look so magical. Icicles would hang from the edge of the roof like expensive crystals. Andy and I would play outside until we were frozen, having snowball fights and trying to catch snowflakes on our tongues." She chuckled. "When we finally went inside, Grams would make us hot chocolate while we warmed up in front of the big stone fireplace."

Suddenly a lump formed in her throat. Had she said too much? Jordan couldn't allow Luke to find out about her past. That would destroy any chance of a future with him. And even though Hilldale wasn't that small, the stories of her family's scandal were never far enough away.

"I bet it was a great place to grow up."

A little sadness crept into her voice. "It was."

Luke noticed her tone had changed. "What's wrong?"

"Nothing, really." She instantly scanned her thoughts, separating what details she felt safe sharing and what ones she couldn't. "It's just that reminiscing about my childhood makes me realize that life will never be that simple and carefree again. But also happy, thinking about the wonderful times I spent with my grandmother."

He saw the light returned to Jordan's eyes along with a childlike expression of pure wonderment. "What are some of your other favorite memories of her?"

"Oh, the holidays were the best! You should have seen all the decorations! Hand-made snowflakes that Andy and I had cut out of paper hung everywhere. The house was transformed beyond imagination. There was garland wrapped around the banister of the stairs and colorful glass balls sat in bowls with sprigs of pine on all the tables. Snow-men and Santa figurines were placed wherever Grams could find a spot. Christmas was a big deal.

"Ever since we were little, my brother and I would stand or kneel on a chair next to the kitchen counter and Grams would let us help frost and put sprinkles her homemade sugar cookies. There were trees and bells and angels and stars. No matter how messy they looked, she always told us what a great job we'd done and she would proudly offer them to guests who dropped by. When I got older, she taught me how to make them. It was our special time together.

"About three weeks before Christmas, the whole family would bundle up and go in search of just the right tree. We'd string popcorn and eat cookies while we hung ornaments on the fragrant branches, and it always stood in front of the big picture window next to the fireplace. One year, the stand leaked and left a stain on the wood floor. Grams was not happy about that." Jordan shook her head.

"But I guess my favorite thing was the hand carved nativity that sat in the center of the mantel just above our stockings. I loved to stare at it while Grams read the story from the family Bible right before Andy and I were sent off to bed on Christmas Eve." Jordan's eyes grew misty, the scene in her mind as vivid as if it were yesterday.

Luke could see how much recalling those special moments meant to her. Maybe one day, they could start their own Christmas traditions that would be just as wonderful. "Did your family have big celebrations for birthdays too?"

Jordan smiled as she continued. "As soon as we woke up that day, we would have to stand inside the pantry door in the kitchen and Grams would measure us to see how much we'd grown over the past year. Then later that afternoon, there would be lots of presents and my parents would throw big parties." Her parents. Jordan's insides clenched and she hoped Luke wouldn't ask her about them. *Why aren't I being more careful?* Thankfully, he didn't press her for more details.

"Sounds nice." Luke paused, "By the way, when is your birthday?"

"April twenty-first, but I'm not going to tell you what year," Jordan teased, scrunching up her face.

Something about that date seemed familiar to him, but he couldn't quite place it.

He was certain though he'd heard or seen that date recently.

He shared some of his childhood antics of being a typical rough and tumble boy, fighting and playing with his brother. She laughed at his adventures. He told her about his dad, the good times they'd had together and how hard it had been when he passed away. It was Jordan's turn to cover his hand with hers, a comforting, heartfelt gesture, replacing any need for words. Their eyes communicated a silent understanding. They both had experienced the hurt of losing a cherished loved one. The flapping of the plastic doggie door broke the mood. Odie had returned from another neighborhood romp and joined them on the couch.

Jordan's eyes sparkled with excitement. "Are you ready for the movie? I've wanted to see this one for a while now."

Propping his stocking feet on the coffee table, Luke draped his arm around her shoulder and she cuddled up against him before pushing Play on the remote.

The next thing he knew, he woke up to the sun shining through the living room window. It took a minute for his mind to register where he was and what had happened. Out of the corner of his eye, he could see Odie sitting on the floor just a foot or so from the couch. The dog was staring at him, not in a bad way, but with more of a puzzled expression. It was almost as if he were thinking, *What are you doing here this early?*

He couldn't feel his left arm and that's when he discovered Jordan curled up next to him. They fit together perfectly. Taking great care not to wake her, he brushed back a few wayward strands of silky brown hair that had fallen across her face. She stirred slightly, pulling his right arm tighter around her waist, and sleepily whispered his name. A rush of emotions spread through his chest. Luke realized, at that moment, he'd fallen hopelessly in love with this amazing woman and wanted to wake up with her in his arms every morning. The sight of her lying there made him believe in a future that he hadn't thought was possible and reignited flames of desire.

Leaning over, he whispered in her ear, "Jordan, wake up." She stirred again, but said nothing. He tried once more, a little louder. "Jordan. Wake up, it's morning."

Her eyes fluttered open, squinting around the room, then up at Luke. "What happened? What are you doing here?"

He chuckled. "We must have fallen asleep while watching the movie."

"Oh yeah, the movie." A hint of memory flashed in her mind on her face. She closed her eyes for a second and as the fog started to clear, she continued. "Sorry, you must be pretty uncomfortable squished on the couch with me," she remarked innocently.

A handsome face, complete with dimples, greeted her. "Not really." Luke winked. "You can fall asleep in my arms anytime. I enjoyed waking up to find you snuggled up against me." His breath was warm against her cheek.

Jordan blushed, but had to admit she liked it, too. "Yeah right, I must look awful." She rubbed her fingers under her eyes, positive her mascara was smudged all across her cheeks.

"You look beautiful. But as much as I'm enjoying this, I probably need my arm back so I can get some circulation going again."

Jordan realized she had it pinned under her, "Oh sure, sorry about that."

The pins and needles started almost immediately. Luke shook his arm then started rubbing it to get the painful tingles to stop.

"How about some breakfast?" Jordan attempted to stifle a yawn. "Should I whip something up here or do you want to go the pancake house down the street?

A slow, sensuous grin lifted the corners of his lips. "Like I said last night, I'd rather help you cook." He added a wiggle of his eyebrows for emphasis.

Jordan playfully rested her hands on her hips. "Ah huh, I saw how you *helped*. We're going out and *you're* buying me breakfast."

He feigned disappointment then leaped to his feet and chased her around the house, her squeals of joy mixing with his hearty bursts of laughter. When he caught her, she didn't hesitate to throw her arms around his neck as he wrapped her in a tender embrace.

Odie padded over to them, blinking his eyes and wondering what all the ruckus was about. The dog looked from one human to the other before deciding he had better go out into the backyard and perform his morning patrol of the fence line. He couldn't be too careful with that sneaky cat, Barney, lurking about the neighborhood.

Later that night at his house, Luke was getting ready for bed and accidentally knocked some books off the end table.

When he bent down, he noticed the old journal had fallen open to the inscription page on the inside front cover. When he picked it up, he stared in disbelief. It wasn't possible, was it? There, in faded ink was the date— *April 21st.*

His mind raced as bits and pieces of his conversations with Jordan were like flashing neon signs in his brain. *The description of the trees in the backyard...the stone fireplace...the stain on the floor in front of the window...and now the birthdays matched.*

"This is too much to be a coincidence, right?" Luke whispered. "There are a lot of old houses outside of town. It could be any of them, couldn't it?" He reached for the brown leather book and started flipping through the pages to re-read certain passages, on a quest to find out the truth.

With the journal gripped in his hand, he went to his computer to do a title search for the property he'd bought. The first names listed were Edwin and Millie (Shaw) Harper. *The same name.* His palms started to sweat. At another website, he typed in their names and found out that Edwin had died a long time ago, so then he searched for Millie, and found her obituary. *"...survived by her two daughters, Linda (Harper) of Columbus, Ohio; and Rebecca (Harper) Price; along with two grandchildren, Maribel J. Price and Andrew J. Price."*

Confused, his brows drew together. *"Maribel? Who's that?"*

A twinge of relief tried to penetrate his mind, but his heart persisted. After typing in Maribel Price on the keyboard, he found a birth record and a second listing without much description. He clicked the item and as he scanned the words, a cold knot formed in his stomach.

He read it out loud twice, just to make sure. "IT IS HEREBY ORDERED that henceforth Maribel Jordan Price shall be known as JORDAN SHAW." Closing his eyes, Luke leaned back in the chair, his chest heavy from this latest discovery. "It can't be. It just can't be." *The markings on the door-frame in the kitchen—M.J. and A.J.—Jordan and Andy.*

The young woman he'd been reading about from the past and had fallen in love with was the same woman he was in love with today.

His dark eyes focused on the leather book next to his computer.

M.J. and Jordan are the same *person.*

This is Jordan's *journal.*

Chapter 11

Jordan was cooking bacon and eggs early one morning when her phone rang. "Hello."

"Mornin', M.J."

She didn't mind him calling her that when nobody was around, after all, that's the name he grew up calling her. "Hey, little brother. What's new?"

The siblings caught up on each other's lives and made plans to get together for Thanksgiving. "You still dating that Luke guy?" Andy's tone turned more concerned and took on an air of uneasiness.

"Yeah. Why?" Jordan's lips curved upward, pressing her cheek against the phone picturing the handsome face of the man she'd fallen for.

"Just checking up on my big sis." He tried to bluff his way around the real reason why he needed to talk to her.

She knew something wasn't quite right.

"Andy, that's not why you called me this early on my day off. What's really going on?"

He paced around his living room, trying to think of the best way to start the conversation he didn't want to have with his sister. Finally, he released a deep breath. "Okay, here goes. Have you told him about Dad?"

Jordan's heart stopped and she almost dropped the spatula she was holding. "No! Of course not! And I'll do anything to keep him from ever finding out."

Andy tried to reason with her. "Don't you think that's a little unrealistic? He'll have to be told sooner or later. What if you two get married?"

Panic rushed through her at the thought of Luke finding out about her past. "He doesn't need to know. He can't know. It would ruin everything and I won't let that happen."

"Do you really think there's enough people left in Hilldale that care about Dad and what he did after all this time? Are you still convinced that his stupidity will ruin your life? It was a long time ago, M.J. Don't you think you're overreacting just a little?"

"No! It was a horrible thing, Andy. And even though some of the people might not remember or care what happened, there will be those who could stir up a lot of trouble for me."

"Well, then you're not going to like what I have to say," he warned her.

Jordan's pulse quickened. "Why? What's going on?"

"The 'suits' stopped by to see me Friday afternoon at work."

Closing her eyes, she collapsed into the nearest kitchen chair. "Why do they keep harassing us?" her voice trembled. "We don't have a clue where he is."

"I know, but I just wanted to warn you because they will probably be heading your way." At first, there was silence on the other end of the phone, but then Andy heard his sister softly crying. This whole ordeal with their father had been hard on both of them. He wished he could do something to help her, but knew he couldn't. "Are you going to be okay, Sis? Do you need me to come out for a couple of days for moral support in case they show up?"

Jordan cleared her throat before answering, "No. Thanks for offering, but I'll be fine. I appreciate the heads-up."

"Do you ever wonder why Dad chose to do what he did? You know, take the money

and run off like that, abandoning his family?"
The visit from the government agents had
started Andy thinking about the past. He
didn't like having to answer the same questions over and over again. But this time he'd
experienced an unusually strong feeling of resentment in the pit of his stomach and
couldn't shake it. He thought that maybe talking it over with his sister might help.

"I used to, but not so much anymore."
Jordan didn't really want to talk about her father. It was pointless and dredged up pain
she'd rather not deal with.

"Midlife crisis maybe, I don't know." He
shrugged.

"That's a lame excuse," Jordan scoffed. "I
think it was just a simple case of selfishness,
greed, and lust."

"I suppose you're right." He breathed a
sigh into the phone before continuing. "But
we had fun with him when we were kids
though, remember? He used to help us build
snowmen and snow forts. He'd take us ice
skating on the pond just beyond that grove of
trees behind Gram's house." He felt a smile
form on his lips. "On the days when it was
raining or too cold for us to go outside, he'd
play hide and hide and seek or board games

with us inside. And the times when we'd all drive over to the coast for long weekends in the summer and swim in the ocean. Remember how cold the water was? And..." His voice slowly trailed off into a whisper.

Jordan grinned slightly as he talked about their childhood, believing that if she closed her eyes tight, she could almost picture a ten-year old Andy on the other end of the line. Silence embraced them as brother and sister took a few moments, each recalling other fond times with their father.

"If you need me, call me. Promise?"

Her voice was a faint, quivering whisper, "I'll be all right." Jordan wasn't sure if she would be or not, but there was no sense in worrying Andy.

"I'll talk to you soon. Take care of yourself, Sis."

"You, too, little brother."

After she hung up with Andy, Jordan held her head in her hands as the hurt and memories of her dad flooded over her. Maybe it was because she had been older, or maybe it was just the fact of being a female herself, that she'd been more aware of the overwhelming devastation in her mother's eyes. During those first few weeks, she had watched her mom struggle to keep it together. Some days she was barely able to summon the courage to hold her head up in public. Especially on those inescapable occasions when necessity dictated her mom go to the doctor's office or to the mechanic. The worst day had been when her mother went to the bank to see if Daddy had left any money in their joint account. Surprisingly, he had. Maybe somewhere inside him had been an ounce or two of fatherly responsibility that still wanted to see that his children were taken care of. Maybe he felt just a little guilty for abandoning his family. An attempt, Jordan thought, to ease his conscience and convince himself he was doing one last good thing before turning his back on them.

Jordan had buried most of the good memories of her father long ago. It made it easier to deal with her bitterness that way—just like her mother had done. Her mom had put on a brave face after they moved away, but Jordan never saw the spark of true joy return to her mother's eyes. She seemed hollow, withdrawn, and just shuffled through the day-to-day motions of merely existing. People who didn't really know her thought she was a pleasant woman, but quiet.

No, there wasn't any reason for Jordan to reminisce about her childhood with her father. And she was certain she could've banished any memory of his existence in her life from her mind if it wasn't for those annoying FBI agents. As the impact of that statement traveled from her brain to her heart, a single tear betrayed her and trickled down her right cheek.

The next thing she knew, the smoke alarm screamed to life and startled her back to reality. Odie began barking at the shrill noise and Jordan yelled at him to shush. She'd gotten so involved in her conversation with Andy, and thinking about her past, that she'd forgotten about her food. Rushing to the stove, she reached through the smoke and turned off the burners. Now her eggs were charcoal blotches on the bottom of her frying pan and her bacon was burnt into thin black strips. Jordan flung open the back door and waved a dishtowel around trying to clear the smoke out of her kitchen. This morning had been a disaster. She cleaned up the mess, showered, and put on clean clothes before heading down to the nearby cafe. She *needed* coffee and *wanted* pancakes. She'd lost her appetite for bacon and eggs.

After Andy hung up, his thoughts lingered on their conversation. He thought about the way he'd felt the day his mom sat him down on the living room sofa and told him that his dad had left and wasn't coming back. His mother hadn't revealed a lot of the details, but afterwards, he remembered feeling confused and scared. An emptiness had crept into his heart over the next few days. The guy was his dad after all, and he'd loved him, looked up to him, idolized him. The move from Hilldale had happened so quickly and he'd been furious at his mother for making him leave his friends, his baseball team, and Grams.

After he'd become a grown man, he understood and was grateful to her for sparing him the prejudice and backlash from the community as a result of his father's betrayal of their trust.

At first, he'd acted out in anger when they went to live with his aunt and uncle. Andy shook his head remembering what a smart-mouthed brat he'd been. They'd been patient with him, for a while, but about a month after they'd arrived, his uncle took him on a camping trip one weekend. Uncle Vince talked to Andy like a friend would, understanding his situation, but then firmly about his bad behavior, like a father. He'd assured Andy that when they returned home his bad attitude would no longer be tolerated. That weekend, his uncle had showed him how to start a campfire, pitch a tent, and fish, using man-made flies instead of bait. He'd even promised to teach him how to tie a fly when they got home. Andy fell in love with the outdoors from that weekend on. He joined the Boy Scouts and pestered his uncle every weekend during the summer until he promised to take him camping again. It was because of him that Andy started his own outdoor adventure business.

Uncle Vince eventually taught him how to drive, and about girls. He'd explained to Andy that a real man loves and cherishes a woman with all his heart, treating her with kindness and respect. He'd also taught him what it meant to be a man of integrity and honor.

Andy owed a lot to his uncle and even sent him Father's Day cards every year. As an adult now, he'd come to realize that it took much more than just sperm to be a father—a real father. Andy hoped that someday when he had kids, Uncle Vince would be proud of the way he raised them.

❀ ❀ ❀

Around eleven o'clock Thursday morning, Jordan was helping Betti Culpepper pick out flowers for her granddaughter's birthday. To say this particular customer was frugal was an understatement. She was downright cheap— and extremely picky. After an hour of looking at floral books and the same batches of roses, carnations, and daisies over and over, the woman finally made her decision.

Jordan had just completed the sale when the bell jingled above the front door of her shop. When she glanced up to greet her new customer, she froze and felt the blood drain from her face. There stood two men in black suits, white shirts, and dark sunglasses. They were from the FBI. And this was not the first time some of J. Edgar's men had visited her at work. Even though Andy had called Sunday morning to warn her they would be coming, now was a bad time for them to show up—the worst possible time in fact. Betti Culpepper was a sixty-year old widow who just happened to be the biggest busybody and gossip in all of Hilldale.

If she discovered who these men were and why they were here, it would be all over town by tomorrow afternoon. Jordan couldn't let that happen.

Even though her business with Betti was done, the woman wouldn't leave the shop. Instead, she loitered near the artificial plants, and Jordan saw her sneak a peek over her shoulder at the pair of strangers. "Is there anything else I can help you with?" Jordan inquired, hoping the woman would be on her way. But she didn't.

"No, I thought I'd just look around a little before I leave. Go ahead and help your other customers, dear. Don't worry about me." Mrs. Culpepper waved her bony fingers in the air.

The two men approached the counter, but before they could say a word, Jordan motioned for them to follow her into the back room. When she felt reasonably sure that they were outside the scope of Betti's radar, she crossed her arms over her chest and stared at their expressionless faces.

Her pulse raced and her mouth felt as dry as the Sahara desert.

"Why do you people keep hassling me?" she whispered firmly. "I've told you before, I don't know anything about the money my father took or where he might be."

"Ms. Shaw, we are just doing our job," the taller of the two men commented as if the answer was obvious. "We need to follow up with you from time to time in case you've had any contact with him," he said, his voice stiff, his tone matter-of-fact—typical FBI. His partner stood next to him like a statue, not saying a word.

Jordan's eyes narrowed, darting from one man to the other, her image reflected in the dark lens of their sunglasses. "Trust me, if I knew where you could find him, I wouldn't hesitate to let you know."

"Ms. Shaw, we've received a tip that there's a possibility he may have returned to the area."

Jordan thought she was going to faint. "*Here*...in Hilldale?"

"Yes, ma'am. We're unclear as to what could be important enough to bring him out of hiding, especially for him to risk coming back here."

"I haven't seen him or heard from him," Jordan said, her voice trembling. "I promise I'll call you if he does get in contact with me, or if I see him around town."

"We would really appreciate it. Also, it is imperative that you don't tell him we were here to see you or that we were asking about him."

"Of course," Jordan responded. "If you *do* find him, will you please let me know?"

"I'll see what I can do, Ms. Shaw. Thank you for your time."

Reaching inside the front of his suit jacket, the man who had done all the talking handed her a business card. "If you do hear from your father, please call this number."

Jordan had seen more than her share of these cards over the years and shoved it in the back pocket of her jeans. "Fine. Now, please leave." Extending her left arm, she pointed her index finger toward the back door. The two agents turned and, with quiet but purposeful strides, walked out. Jordan released a silent prayer that if the town gossip was still lurking in the front of the shop, she hadn't heard the conversation.

Jordan rounded the corner to go check on Betti and found that, indeed, the woman had crept closer to the entrance of the workroom. Since Jordan was wearing tennis shoes, her sudden appearance startled Mrs. Culpepper. The blue vase in Betti's hands teetered for a moment before she placed it back on the glass display shelf then self-consciously straightened her skirt. The gesture, along with the look on the older woman's face told Jordan that she was slightly embarrassed, not because of her eavesdropping, but because she'd been caught.

"Those men looked like they meant business, dear. Is everything all right?" Betti inquired. Her tone was overly sweet with concern as she flashed Jordan one of her more sincere-looking, but fake, smiles.

"There's nothing to worry about, Mrs. Culpepper."

"Who are they? Did they leave?" Betti stood on her tiptoes, trying to peer over Jordan's shoulder. "I didn't see them walk back this way? I hope you're not in some sort of trouble," the busybody continued.

Jordan had to bite her tongue but knew just what to say in order to make the older woman leave without any further interrogation. "I see you like this vase. Did you want me to add it on to your previous purchase?"

Disappointment showed in Mrs. Culpepper's eyes. She'd been unsuccessful at garnering any valuable information from Jordan about the two mysterious men, or the reason for their visit. "Oh, no. I was just looking. I best be on my way," she replied before turning toward the door. "Now remember, deary, use only the *freshest* flowers in my granddaughter's arrangement."

"I will, Betti. Have a good afternoon."

Jordan was thankful that Mrs. Culpepper had finally gone. There was nothing she could do but wait to see if people in town started whispering as she walked by. It wouldn't take long to learn if Betti had heard anything.

What if they'd come to the house when Luke was there? A cold shiver ran down her spine at the possibility.

That would have ruined everything.

Chapter 12

Luke and Jordan got together early Sunday morning and packed a picnic lunch, fishing poles and doggie essentials for Odie. They drove out of town for about an hour or so to a beautiful park near a small lake. The two humans took turns entertaining their furry companion by tossing Frisbees, balls, and playing tug of war with a braided cloth rope.

A red and black Pendleton blanket lay on the grass under the tall oak where Luke and Jordan ate fried chicken, potato salad, and buttermilk biscuits. Odie had his food, but Luke managed to sneak him a bite or two of meat when his owner wasn't looking. After they'd put everything away except the blanket, Jordan leaned against the tree. Luke stretched out on his back with his head resting in her lap. A light breeze blew through the branches as he closed his eyes while she ran her fingers slowly through his hair. They talked about little things, but mostly they sat quietly, relaxing, and just enjoyed being together.

Jordan loved him so much, it scared her how deep her feelings were for this handsome man with his dark bedroom eyes and sinful smile. His hair was thick, but soft beneath her hand. She hadn't been this happy in a very long time.

Luke was almost asleep when suddenly a mixture of loud squawks and barks tore through the tranquility. Jumping to his feet, he instantly saw the source of the noise. Odie was chasing the ducks up and down the edge of the lake.

Occasionally a large, white goose would turn the tables and chase him, trying to nip the dog's hindquarters. Luke and Jordan roared with laughter, holding their sides, but eventually decided they should go rescue the ducks from Odie, and Odie from the goose.

Luke grabbed Jordan and threatened to toss her in the water, but she flashed him a "don't you dare" warning and he reconsidered his playful prank.

Deciding not to fish after all, they dangled their feet off the edge of the dock for a while. About mid-afternoon, he turned to her. "Do you want to head back? We could go see that movie you mentioned the other day."

"I'd love to. You're not too tired?"

He gently placed his lips on hers, drawing her against him. "I'm never too tired to spend time with you."

Jordan melted inside every time he kissed her.

They packed up the truck and hoisted Odie into the back seat. Luke stopped at Jordan's to drop off the dog and give her a chance to change clothes before they drove to his place so he could freshen up.

It had been about half an hour since Luke had disappeared down the hall. When Jordan went to find him, she heard sounds coming from his bedroom. As she was about to knock and go in, she realized he was on the phone. Before she could turn and leave, she overheard part of what Luke was saying and it stopped her in her tracks.

"...no, she doesn't have a clue what I'm up to....my plans to move are coming along great...I can't wait to get out of here...I can always use the extra money...with your help, that old book...all I need for a new beginning."

Leave? Where is he going? Why hasn't he

said anything to me about it? Jordan quietly retraced her steps back to the living room. Confused and partly ashamed for eaves dropping on Luke's conversation, she wasn't paying attention to where she was going and bumped into the side table next to the couch. Papers and magazines spilled onto the floor. Squatting down, she began picking up the mess when the worn edge of a brown book caught her attention. The hairs on the back of her neck stood up, alarm shivered down her spine.

Jordan hesitated, her body paralyzed for several seconds. With shaking, tentative hands she reached for the book as if approaching a growling dog or a coiled snake. Her instincts warned her that pain was imminent should she decide to proceed. After sliding away the magazine that lay on top of it, she felt the color drain from her face, and for a second, she thought she might faint. It was her old journal from years ago, the one that held her most personal thoughts—and secrets.

When her fingertips came in contact with the leather cover, a rush of memories poured into her mind. *Grams—young, innocent love—heartache—abandonment.* Drawing in a deep breath, and with trembling fingers, she lifted the journal so she could examine it more closely. Fear insisted she prove it to her eyes, even though her heart knew without a doubt it was hers. Carefully, Jordan opened the cover, revealing the dedication in her mother's distinctive handwriting. Closing the lost treasure, she clutched it to her chest as visions of the past clouded her eyes and tears streamed down her face. Sobbing uncontrollably as the emotions resurrected from the simple leather book took hold, she gathered all her strength just to stand. *Why does Luke have this? How did he get it?* Panic swept through her. *Did he read it? Did he figure out that it belonged to me? Did he discover the family secret I've been running from all these years?*

Noises down the hall reminded her of the conversation she'd overheard. '*...she doesn't have a clue...old book...leaving...money...*' Anger instantly replaced her tears.

A moment later, Luke walked into the room and found Jordan holding her old journal. He could tell she'd been crying and panic gripped his heart like a vice. "Jordan, let me explain—"

"Where did you get this?" Shock and anger filled her eyes as she looked up at him.

Her piercing gaze locked on his face, demanding the truth.

Luke exhaled deeply, lowered his eyes, and ran his fingers through his hair, scrambling for an explanation. He couldn't say anything for a long minute. An agonizingly long minute for Jordan.

"I heard you on the phone just now," she informed him when she didn't get a response,

"You weren't supposed to hear any of that. The guy on the phone is a friend of mine—"

"So that makes it okay? Why were you discussing my journal with him? Are you conspiring with him on what's the best way to make a few dollars by digging up my family's scandal and publicly humiliating me?" The intensity of her stare drilled a hole right through him.

"What are you talking about?" Images flashed through Luke's mind. *Brad—Her father—Changing her name.* He tried again. "It's not what you think. Please listen, my love—"

"Don't call me that!" Jordan spat out the words, tossing him a look that made his blood run cold. "Is this what all the questions were about the other night? Did you need more details on my family to make the story better? Did you enjoy playing me for a fool?"

Her throat muscles constricted making it difficult to speak. Luke watched as tears slid down her cheeks. "I trusted you. How could you do this to me?" Her shoulders sagged, hurt and disbelief etched on her face.

"I wouldn't do that." The muscles in his stomach clenched at the wounded look in her eyes. Worse yet, she blamed him for being the cause of her pain. He frantically searched his mind for the words to convince her, but he didn't really know what to say.

"Why should I believe you? You've obviously been lying to me all along." Raw emotions etched lines across her face as trembling fingers wiped the dampness from her cheeks.

"That's not true! I love you—" he protested, growing more frustrated with their conversation minute by minute.

"Don't!" she screamed at him. "Don't you ever say that to me again!" Jordan hurled the journal at his head. He ducked just in time before hearing it thud against the wall behind him. Then, grabbing her purse, she ran for the front door.

"Jordan, wait!"

"No, Luke, I won't. We're done. Don't

call me and don't stop by the shop. I don't ever want to see you again!" Flinging the door open, she bolted out of his house.

Luke stood there a moment, stunned and unable to move. When he heard Jordan's car start, he ran outside to stop her, but it was too late. The tires screeched on the pavement as she sped away down the street and he watched her taillights fade into the night. A blue streak of swear words spewed from his lips, the kind that would've made any sailor proud. He went back inside, slamming the door behind him. Luke stomped over to where the book lay open on the floor. He felt like he'd been punched in the gut—hard. *Now what? How am I going to fix this? How am I going to make her understand?*

Jordan parked her SUV in the garage, unsure how she'd managed to make it home without crashing. As she turned off the engine, she buried her face in both hands and wept uncontrollably for several minutes. Her initial fears about him had been true. Handsome, smooth-talking men like Luke Kincaid were not to be trusted. The distant sound of barking made its way through the fog of pain. Odie. He'd heard the car and was waiting inside for her.

Her body felt as if it weighed a thousand pounds as she shuffled around her kitchen. She filled the dog's food bowl and placed it on the floor, before struggling down the hall and into her room. Odie sensed something was wrong, but right now, the grumbling of his stomach was his first priority. He'd go check on his owner *after* dinner.

Jordan crawled onto her bed, clothes and all, pulling Gram's handmade quilt over on top of her weary body. She was numb at first, but as the conversation with Luke re-played in her mind, the unbearable heartache took hold. Once again, the sobs could not be restrained and her body shook as she released the devastating feelings of humiliation and betrayal.

Unnoticed by his owner, Odie padded into Jordan's bedroom. He stared at her, tilting his head one way and then the other before releasing a small whimper of concern. When she didn't respond, he curled up on the rug beside her bed and waited, just in case she needed him. Darkness filled the room and sleep soon claimed them both.

Luke couldn't calm down after Jordan left. He paced the floor for what seemed like hours.

His mind was numb, unable to concentrate. His thoughts were muddled and bounced around in his head. Chaos reigned in Luke's world tonight. Eventually, he slept, more from exhaustion than by choice.

When he woke up the next morning, he hoped that it had been just a bad dream. But the pile of magazines that lay scattered on the living room floor along with the small dent in the far wall was all the evidence he needed to prove him wrong. To say things hadn't worked out quite the way he'd planned, would be like saying Alaska gets only a "dusting" of snow every winter. He felt drained and had no idea how to repair the damage that had been done here just a few hours ago.

The next morning when Jordan opened her eyes, the memory of last night flooded over her. A heavy weight settled in her stomach and tangled emotions clutched at her heart. She knew there was absolutely no way she could function enough to go to work today. Around eight-thirty, she picked up the phone and called Helen. Her dear friend was always willing to help Jordan whenever she needed a day off or had to go away on business. Being a retired schoolteacher, Jordan's friend was usually available on short notice. Helen was more than willing to work for the next couple of days so Jordan could stay home and rest—while fighting "the flu." The terrible events at Luke's house filled her every waking moment and grew more overwhelming as the day progressed.

By Tuesday, she was at least able to summon the strength and desire to take a shower and perform basic household tasks. She even watched a couple of old movies, comedies of course. She was careful not to select ones that contained any sort of relationships in them— not even a tiny kiss.

Random, unannounced episodes of sadness snuck up on her and tears fell throughout the day, but not like the body consuming sobs she'd experienced the other night. Luke's face was always present in her mind—but so was what he'd done.

Chapter 13

About a week after their fight, Jordan was doing her best to maintain her composure at work even though it took every ounce of strength she had. Tears always lay in wait and only a millisecond away from eroding the façade she'd created. Some days the hurt was bearable, other days it was relentless—today was one of those days.

With just an hour to go, Jordan was relieved that soon, she could find solace, once again, in the comfort and safety of her queen-sized bed, shutting out the world. Taking a deep breath, she dusted the display shelves and swept the floor, anything to make the minutes tick by faster. The next time she peered up at the clock above the cash register, a wave of relief washed over her—it was time to go home. She'd made it.

But her feeling of accomplishment was short lived. As she was locking the front door and turning the sign around to indicate the shop was now closed, movement outside the large window caught her attention. A couple stood pointing through the glass at the different arrangements, arms wrapped around each other. From the joyful expressions on their faces, it was obvious to Jordan that they were in love. The happy pair couldn't see her, and even if they had known she was there, she didn't believe it would've made a difference. Her stomach twisted remembering how *she* felt when Luke had gazed at her like that. Closing her eyes, she tried to fight down the heartache welling up within her. When Jordan looked through the glass again, she witnessed the young couple sharing a tender kiss. Her knees began to tremble, a stabbing pain tore at her heart, and for a moment, she wasn't sure if she had the strength to make it out to her vehicle.

Lying in bed that night, she wondered if her body would react this way every time she had an appointment with an elated bride-to-be or had to create beautiful flowers for a romantic wedding. The powerful agony in Jordan's heart held her captive when darkness surrounded her, especially when the sleep she craved and needed eluded her. Tears had become her constant companion. Turning the radio on next to her bed, she hoped the mellow music would help lull her away from reality. After a day filled with physical and emotional stress, it didn't take long before her breathing became slow and even, and she slept. Jordan called Helen on Wednesday morning and asked for her help again. Helen asked a few questions, expressing concern for her friend's health, but Jordan dodged them successfully. Helen offered to bring her some homemade chicken noodle soup from the café down the street. Jordan thanked her, but politely said that it wasn't necessary. She didn't feel like eating. Her appetite had been nonexistent the last few days, so she decided to go back to bed. She prayed for sleep—but this time, it didn't come. Instead, she replayed the moments of the night when she found out Luke had her journal. Every movement, every word, every detail taunted her relentlessly. When she couldn't stand the turmoil any longer, she surrendered to a thought that had been gently nudging her the last few hours. She'd tried to dismiss it as nonsense, but eventually she felt this was the only thing left to try. It was crazy, but she didn't have any other ideas. Somewhere she managed to find the energy to shower and change clothes before making a quick stop by a roadside market on the edge of town.

Silence surrounded Jordan as she drove down the two-lane, country road. It had been a lot of years since she'd driven to this part of town. A bundle of yellow daisies lay in the passenger seat. She continued to wrestle with the idea of whether or not to come here today. It seemed a little odd, but just talking to someone she trusted might help clear her head.

After finding the number she was looking for, Jordan parked her vehicle and slid out from behind the steering wheel. The well-manicured lawn was green and lush, cushioning her tentative steps. Colorful flowers dotted the area and mature trees provided shade for those hot summer afternoons.

When she reached her destination, she took a deep breath and placed the daisies in the vase. "I hope you like these. I remember they were your favorite." Jordan eased herself down on the grass next to the woman whose advice she'd come for. "My life's a mess. I wish you hadn't made me come back to this town for my inheritance. It's only caused me more stress." She paused for a moment, absently plucking a few random blades of grass nearby. "I'm sorry. I know my problems aren't your fault.

"I've fallen in love with a man, but he found out about Daddy and the family scandal. We had a terrible fight." Her whole body tensed, recalling that horrible night, and her folded hands trembled in her lap.

"I heard him talking to someone on the phone and he's going to sell the story to some tabloid. I'll have to put my shop up for sale and move away—everyone will know." Her voice quivered as a tear trickled down her cheek. She didn't want to leave Hilldale and her friends. A strange twinge told her that even after all that had happened, a part of her would miss Luke, too. "I need your help. What should I do?" she pleaded, but there was no response. "I really wish you were here, Grams." She felt a little silly saying that out loud to her grandmother's headstone.

Jordan sat there a while longer; quiet, just remembering the love this woman had given so unselfishly to her family. Happiness and warmth spread through her. Suddenly she imagined Grams doing her best to convince God for permission to send her a hug, because that's what it felt like. Loving arms wrapping around her, comforting her, and letting her know deep inside that things would be all right. Jordan had to chuckle picturing that conversation—her feisty grandmother and The Almighty.

"Bye, Grams. I love you and I miss you so much." Placing a kiss on her fingertips, she pressed them against the cold granite in front of her. Just as she got up to leave, she heard a woman's voice behind her.

"Jordan?"

When she turned around, her heart leapt into her throat. There stood Anna Kincaid.

"I'm sorry, I didn't mean to interrupt. I was on my way to visit my husband, Edward."

Finding it difficult to breathe, Jordan scrabbled for a response. "Um...no...I was just leaving."

"You were visiting Millie, I see. She was quite a woman."

Jordan's eyes flew open. "You—you knew my grandmother?"

"Yes, I did. You must be Rebecca's daughter.

At that moment, Jordan prayed the ground under her feet would open up and swallow her whole.

Luke's mom knew her family! Did he tell her? Did he let his mom read her journal? How much more humiliating could this situation get? "Yes," she whispered. "So I suppose you know all about...you know."

"Your father, and the money, and running off with another woman? Yes, I know." Anna's tone was soft and empathetic. "It was a terrible time for your mother, but I remember how brave she was. We hadn't lived here very long before she packed you and your brother up and moved away."

Tears formed in Jordan's eyes, even though she hadn't heard any judgment or condemnation in Anna's voice. "You must be relieved that Luke and I broke up then?"

"Why would you say that?" Confusion formed on the older woman's face. "And what would any of this have to do with Luke?"

"The scandal, the tainted reputation of my family. I'm sure that's not what you want for your son."

Anna laughed slightly then saw the hurt look in Jordan's eyes. "I'm sorry. I'm not making fun of your past. Please, come sit with me on that bench over there and I'll tell you what I think."

Even though she wasn't quite sure why, Jordan agreed.

"First off," Anna said, looking tenderly into the younger woman's face, "Luke does what he wants. In case you haven't figured it out yet, he's pretty hard-headed."

Tiny wrinkle lines appeared at the corners of Jordan's eyes as her lips twitched, obviously realizing the truth of that statement. "Yeah, I've noticed," she responded while wiping her cheeks.

"Second, I have no reason to judge you because of what your father did years ago." She smiled and saw Jordan relax a little. "Besides, I didn't even know you two had broken up. Luke doesn't make a habit of sharing the details of his personal life with me. Did something happen? Does he know about your family?"

Jordan felt her body tense again. "Yes, he knows."

"And you think he'd hold it against you?"

"Of course!" She wasn't going to go into detail with Luke's mom about the conversation she'd overheard. "Your family is well respected in this community. If people found out who I really am, the scandal would be the hottest topic around town again."

"Luke doesn't care about those old fools who have nothing better to do than gossip. And neither do I." Anna placed her hand over Jordan's, giving them a little squeeze.

"Really?"

"Absolutely. We believe it's what's on the inside of a person that matters, not a lot of nonsense about the sins of the father."

Jordan couldn't believe her ears. Anna sincerely didn't seem to care about what her father had done.

The two women talked a while longer and Jordan found out how Anna knew the story of her family. Anna had volunteered in the assisted living facility where her grandmother had lived for a few years after Jordan's mother moved back East. Grams had confided in Anna about her son-in-law. They'd laughed together and cried together and became good friends before Millie passed away.

"Whatever happened to your grandmother's house?" Anna asked.

"I was saving up for the down payment, but when I went to the bank to ask for an extension, Mr. Armbrewster told me they'd sold it two weeks earlier to someone else." Sadness welled up in her heart. "My grandfather built that house before I was born and I had really hoped to be able to fix it up and live there again someday."

"I'm sorry, dear. That bank manager is an old stick in the mud. He likes to wield his authority around. His only concern is money, not people. Did you ask him who bought it? Maybe they would sell it to you," Anna suggested.

"No, I don't want to know. I guess things don't always work out like you planned," she said with a shrug.

Jordan thought about their conversation all the way home that afternoon. Luke's mom was a special woman. It was nice to be able to share stories about her grandmother with someone who had known her and cared about her.

Doubt and fear didn't stay away for long. Jordan thought about what Anna had said regarding Luke. Everything she'd heard him say on the phone that night was contrary to what his mother told her. Did Anna have blinders on where her son was concerned? He'd said he was leaving. He was plotting behind her back to humiliate her. Luke Kincaid was not the person his mother thought he was. Even if they gave their relationship another try, Jordan was positive that her past would drive them apart eventually. She might as well accept the fact there was no future for them.

Her initial instinct about him had been true. She should have listened to her gut. Well, she'd know better next time. A chill raced up her spine.

Next time? No, she'd been burned enough and she'd finally learned her lesson—there would be no "next time." She wouldn't allow it.

Chapter 14

Several days after the fight with Jordan, Luke was trying to get some chores done around his house. But in the last hour, the only thing he'd accomplished was to pace from one room to another, his thoughts monopolized by the woman he loved. Finally, he grabbed the phone and dialed her number.

"Hello."

"Jordan, I need to talk to you." His tone was determined, but not demanding.

Fear gripped her heart at the sound of his voice. "I told you not to call me."

"How can I convince you that there's been a huge misunderstanding?" Luke wanted so much for her to believe him, but sounds of her weeping softly filtered through the phone. "What can I say to make things better between us?"

Jordan wounds were still raw from his cruel and selfish betrayal. "Nothing. There's nothing you can say. I told you it's over."

Before he could plead his case any further, the dial tone buzzed in his ear.

Luke dealt with the situation the only way he knew how, the way he'd done before when life had knocked him to his knees. He escaped into his work. Renovating the old house helped relieve some of the stress and pent up frustration inside him. Long, hard hours of manual labor, many days to the point of exhaustion, was his solution. Walls were painted in half the time, and with every swing of the hammer, nails were driven in faster than usual.

When Luke finally did go home at the end of the day, he'd force himself to eat a little something, strictly out of necessity, then shower and fall into bed—praying that he wouldn't dream about Jordan. His prayers too often went unanswered.

Fatigue caused his mind to wander one night while repairing a bookshelf in the study of Jordan's childhood home. His thoughts focused on the gut-wrenching pain in her eyes and the anger on her face the night she'd found the journal. The memory cut straight through him. He swung the hammer, missed the nail, and hit his thumb. Shaking his injured hand, he let go a string of the best cuss words he knew. It was time to call it a night. Not paying attention in his business was dangerous.

He struggled to get himself out of bed for work the next morning. These grueling fourteen and fifteen hour days were starting to take their toll on him. His plan wasn't working, the restlessness inside him still refused to die. Maybe he should talk to someone who could help him sort things out and give him a fresh perspective. But who? Who could he confide in? Philip? Definitely not the guys at work. Luke released a deep breath and rubbed his hand down his weary, stubbled face. He called his office to tell them he'd be in later then stumbled to the shower.

A half an hour later, he picked up the phone. "Hey, it's me. Do mind if I stop by this morning?"

"No, not at all."

"Okay, then, I'll see you soon." Luke grabbed a cup of coffee at one of those drive-through places on his way across town.

She heard his truck pull up and was waiting for him at the front door. "What's going on?"

Luke leaned over and placed a kiss on her cheek as he walked in the door. "Hi, Mom."

Thursday morning Darcy called in sick, so Jordan had to make the deliveries. Right before her last stop, she called Peterson's Garage and spoke with Jimmy. He was the mechanic who usually worked on the van for the flower shop, as well as on her personal vehicle. Arriving shortly after three o'clock, she drove into the garage's gravel parking lot. It was time for basic maintenance. The oil needed to be changed and the tires rotated. Jimmy emerged from one of the two open bays wearing his greasy, blue one-piece overalls and wiping his hands on a dirty, red rag. He waved then motioned to where he wanted her to park.

Jordan stepped out of the van and handed over the keys. "Thanks for getting me in on such short notice." She smiled when she noticed a dark smudge on Jimmy's right cheek. He'd always looked young for his age, but right now he reminded her of a little boy who'd been "helping" his dad work on a car.

While she waited, Jordan relaxed on the

bench outside enjoying the gorgeous fall weather. A faint breeze brushed across her face. This was her favorite time of year. Some of the nearby trees had donned their autumn wardrobes of yellows, oranges, and reds. They stood sprinkled among the pines, creating a vivid and picturesque landscape, like the ones on postcards and calendars.

On his way back to his office, Luke noticed the gas gauge was getting close to empty on the work truck he was driving. After pulling into the nearest station, he reached down and pushed the lever to pop open the fuel cover. Suddenly, he caught a familiar silhouette out of the corner of his eye. He glanced in that direction. It was Jordan. Every cell in his body came alive. Luke hadn't seen her since she'd stormed out of his house. She looked beautiful. Soft rays from the afternoon sun filtered through the trees, shimmering off her silky brown hair.

Jordan hadn't paid any attention to the truck that pulled up next to the gas pumps a few feet away. She'd been busy making notes on her to-do list for tomorrow.

Boots scuffed on the gravel next to her, and then she heard a deep male voice. "Hello, Jordan."

Her head shot up and she was instantly overcome by conflicting emotions. Her heart skipped a beat at the sight of his handsome face, but her mind stayed focused, recalling the memory of what he'd done. Her lips thinned out as she glared up at him. "Mr. Kincaid." She witnessed the muscle in his jaw twitch at the formal greeting right before he turned and walked away. It was a good thing she was sitting down. Luke could still make her blood race through her veins, no matter what had happened between them.

He returned to the truck. It was obvious that Jordan's attitude toward him hadn't changed. He hadn't been living under the delusion that she'd all of a sudden get over how angry she'd been. Especially since she'd refused to talk to him the couple of times he'd tried to call her. Still, he had hoped that maybe once she'd cooled off and had a chance to think about what he'd said, she'd at least give him a chance to explain. With a quick peek over his shoulder at her, he watched the beautiful woman who irritated him and rattled his senses, but she was ignoring him. He'd just finished paying the attendant when the twittering sound of a phone caught his attention. Luke checked to make sure it wasn't his work cell or his personal one. Looking around, he noticed Jordan retrieve her phone from the pocket of her jacket, followed by a faint hello. His fingers were just lifting the door handle when he heard her gasp.

"What?...Oh my, God!" She jumped to her feet as a look of panic swept over her face.

Luke stood still, staring at her. He should leave, but he couldn't, not yet.

"Absolutely, whatever you think is best." She was pale and it appeared the person on the other end of the line was doing most of the talking. Her palm rested flat on her chest as she nodded. "Of course...Thank you so much for calling...Okay, I'll be there as soon as I can." When Jordan turned around, Luke's eyes locked with hers. Trails of tears glistened on her cheeks.

Sprinting back into the garage, she began yelling frantically at the mechanic. "Jimmy! Get my van down! Something horrible has happened and I have to leave right now!"

He gave her a puzzled expression. "I'm sorry, Jordan. I can't do that." He gestured toward the dark amber-colored oil dripping from the underside of the van. "The soonest I can get you out of here is about twenty minutes."

Jordan waved her arms around. "I can't wait that long! I have to go!" she screamed through her tears. Her voice quivered. Frustrated, she shook her head and flung her arms down along the sides of her body, like a small child throwing a temper tantrum.

Luke knew he should mind his own business. *Just get in the truck. It's not your problem. She doesn't want anything to do with you.* His head was trying to convince him to do the sensible thing, but his heart was concerned. He needed to know why she was so upset. After a moment, he walked over to where she and Jimmy were standing. "Jordan, what's wrong?"

Taken by surprise, she spun toward him. She didn't have time to deal with her feelings for him right now. She had more urgent things to worry about.

"Oh hey, Luke." Jimmy nodded, hoping his buddy could help him convince this hysterical female he couldn't do what she wanted. "I'm trying to explain to her that I can't give her the van right now. I'm in the middle of the oil change and two of the tires are already off." The mechanic jerked his permanently, grease-stained thumb over his left shoulder.

It was Jordan's turn to plead her case as if Luke was refereeing this debate. "And I'm telling *him* that I have an emergency. I need my van. Now!" After taking a deep breath, she continued. "Not that it's really any of your business, Mr. Kincaid." A mixture of anger and fear showed in her aqua eyes.

Jimmy's eyebrows shot up as he looked at Luke. It was clear that his friend had done something to piss off the woman standing between them. Jimmy had seen that expression and heard that tone of voice from his wife a time or two. It was never good.

When Luke turned back to Jordan, he could see her face had softened a little as tears pooled in her eyes. "What happened?" he asked taking a step closer to her.

"It's Odie! He's been hurt! Someone found him and took him to the vet's office. They think he may have been hit by a car." Covering her face with both hands, Jordan broke down. "I have to get to him!" *Why did* he *have to be the one who stopped at* this *garage*? She didn't want him to see her like this. Scared. Crying. Fragile.

Luke knew how much that little dog meant to her. "I'll take you," he offered, gently cupping her elbow. A tight knot formed in his stomach. He'd grown fond of Odie during the time he'd spent building the shed in Jordan's backyard. He recalled laughing at how ferociously the pup had defended his territory, especially from any feline that happened to trespass on top of *his* fence. The cats weren't intimidated by his growling and barking, though. So when they'd had enough of his antics, they'd leisurely stretch all four legs before disappearing to go find a new source of entertainment. Odie would strut around the yard, his head held high, proud that he'd successfully defeated the enemy.

Jordan yanked her arm free from his grasp. "I don't want to go anywhere with you," she snapped while trying to pull herself together. Whirling around, she faced Jimmy. Aggravated, her impatience flared again as she pointed up. "That's why I need my van! Can't you just throw the tires back on? Shove the plug back in and toss in a couple quarts of oil. I need to leave!"

Luke didn't know why he was putting himself in the middle of this situation. Then his heart reminded him, *It's because you love her.* "Jordan," he said, his tone soft, but firm. "Jimmy told you he won't have it ready for a while. He can't just stop in the middle of what he's doing. Just come with me and I'll drive you to the vet's."

Jordan glared back and forth between the two men. Why were they giving her such a hard time? These stupid men didn't understand how much she loved that little dog. She *needed* to get to Odie.

Luke's voice remained calm as he tried to reason with her. "You really don't have any other choice if you want to get to him right away."

Her shoulders drooped and she looked as if she was about to burst into tears again. Desperate to get to her injured pet, she finally agreed. If accepting help from him was the only way, then that was a sacrifice she was willing to make—but she didn't have to like it. "Fine." She spun around and stomped toward the truck. When she pulled open the passenger door, an empty soda can rolled out and pinged against the gravel. There were papers, fast food bags, and wrappers all over.

"What a mess," she barked at him.

"It's my work truck." He scowled while removing the trash so she could climb in. "I'm sorry if the seats aren't made of Italian leather, the door handles aren't gold plated, and there aren't plush mats on the floor." He didn't mean to be quite so harsh with her, but her attitude annoyed him, especially when all he was trying to do was help her. As they drove down the road, Jordan dabbed at her eyes all the way to the vet's office, but she wouldn't look at him or utter a single word.

He wasn't sure what to say, or if he should even say anything. So he decided to say nothing. The truck had barely pulled up to the curb in front of the vet's office when she flung open the door and rushed inside the building. He sat there for a few moments longer, debating whether to follow her—at least to check on Odie. She had made it crystal clear that *she* didn't want his company.

By the time he'd parked and walked inside, the vet, Dr. Leonard, was speaking with Jordan. Luke stood quietly off to the side hoping to hear what had happened to the dog.

"I've finished my initial exam and we took some x-rays," the vet told her. "So far it doesn't appear he's suffered any internal injuries, but he does have a broken leg."

Crying softly, Jordan closed her eyes for a few seconds. "My poor little guy," she whispered before focusing her blurry vision back to the vet's face. "Can I see him?"

"I'll go check to see if they're done cast-

ing his leg yet. We gave him some pain med-
ication, but I want to keep him overnight for
observation. I also want to run some more
tests in the morning just to be sure he doesn't
develop any new symptoms or complica-
tions."

Dr. Leonard was Odie's regular vet, so she
knew him and his history. She placed her
hand on Jordan's arm. "He's strong and
healthy. So at this point, I have no doubt that
he'll be back to his old self before too long."
Then the doctor disappeared behind a door
marked, "Employees Only."

When Jordan turned around, she was startled to see Luke standing there.

"It's sounds like he's going to be okay."
He could see a wide range of emotions playing across her face: fear—and sadness for her
dog mixed with the resentment she still felt
toward him. "He's a tough little guy," he
added.

Jordan nodded while patting her eyes and
cheeks with a crumpled tissue. Luke didn't
know what to do next. Part of him command-
ed his legs to turn around and leave. But his
heart insisted he stay with her until she could
go back to see Odie. No matter what had
happened that night at his house, he had sym-

pathy for her and what she was going through. Deciding it would be best if he left after all, he took a step toward the door, but she stopped him.

"Please don't go, Luke. I'm scared." Her voice trembled as she gazed into his warm brown eyes. "What if they find something else wrong? What if he doesn't make it?"

A new stream of tears flowed over her bottom lashes as she stepped into his waiting arms. Sobbing against his broad shoulder, some of Jordan's stress melted away. She'd always felt safe wrapped in his strong embrace. He whispered words of comfort and encouragement while he helped her to a chair in the waiting room. "You heard the doc. He'll be good as new in no time. He'll be chasing Barney out of the backyard before you know it."

In between her tears, Jordan tried to laugh at that picture. "I just don't understand how he got out?" she sniffled.

"Do you want me stop by your house and take a look?"

All of a sudden, a hurtful scene flashed in her mind—Luke had her journal. She straightened and pulled away from him. "No. I'll ah...I'll call and have someone come out to check the fence before I take Odie home."

He'd felt her body tense right before she sat up. He could only assume she'd finally remembered she was still mad at him. "I don't mind, Jordan..."

"I wouldn't want to inconvenience you any more than I have." She blew her nose and he saw the same hardness in her eyes as he'd seen at Peterson's.

"Well then, I better be going," he muttered, as he stood. "I hope Odie will be all right."

He turned to walk away, but she called out to him again. "Luke, wait. Thank you for giving me a ride and for your concern." Her voice was sincere, yet determined. Her eyes focused on his face as she lifted her chin. "But nothing has changed between us."

Before he could respond, Doctor Leonard reappeared. "Jordan, you can come on back now." Jumping to her feet, she followed the vet through the door without even a backwards glance at the man who'd held her so tenderly just a few short minutes ago.

Even though he was a little groggy, Odie swished his tail happily and whimpered at the sight of his owner. One of his front legs was wrapped in a blue cast. Jordan knelt down so she could stroke his tan and white fur, talking softly to the injured dog.

"We'll see how he's doing tomorrow," Dr. Leonard said. "I'll call you and let you know the results of the latest tests. At that time, I'll let you know if he can go home in the afternoon."

"Okay," Jordan whispered, but didn't turn to face the vet. She just stared into the trusting, dark eyes of her furry friend.

"You can stay a little longer, but his pain meds should kick in pretty soon and knock him out," the doctor added.

Jordan sat on the floor right next to Odie until he drifted off to sleep.

After making sure he was settled in, she trudged back to the lobby and approached the front desk. Behind the counter sat a young woman who was talking on the phone, giggling, and twirling the pink streak in her hair. After a couple of minutes, Jordan cleared her throat impatiently. She was tired and she just wanted to go home.

When the receptionist looked up at Jordan, it was clear the interruption to her conversation was not appreciated. "Hey Richie, I'll call you later...Yeah...No really, I gotta go." After setting down her cell phone, she pivoted in her chair, making the small plastic name tag pinned to her shirt visible to Jordan. It read, JILL.

"May I help you?" The dark eyes that stared at Jordan appeared to be anything but helpful.

"My dog was brought in this afternoon—"

"Name?" Jill interrupted and faced the computer, her fingers hovering over the keyboard, black nail polish a sharp contrast against her ivory skin.

"Jordan Shaw."

The young woman tilted her head, a slight scowl of irritation on her face. "The *dog's* name?"

"Oh, sorry. It's been a very long day." Jordan sighed. "His name is Odie. I've forgotten if your office is going to call me or if I should call tomorrow to find out when I can come pick him up?"

Jill's fingernails clicked against the keys. She scanned the monitor and clicked a few more times. "We'll call you after the doc has a chance to check him over."

"Are you going to mail me a bill?"

"No," the young woman informed her. "You'll have to pay the full amount when you come to pick up Ollie."

"Odie," Jordan corrected her.

"What?" Jill asked, confused and annoyed.

"His name is *Odie*." The impatience must have glared from Jordan's eyes, because she could tell her message was received.

The young woman offered an insincere, half smile. "Sorry."

Jordan turned and shuffled across the floor, plopping herself down into a plastic chair by the front door. She was worn out. Pulling out her cell phone, she called Megan. "Hi, it's me. Can you please come pick me up from the vet's office?"

"Are you having car problems?"

"No. Odie got hurt, but the doctor thinks he'll be okay. I'll explain in the car."

"I'll be right there."

"Thanks, I'll see you a few minutes."

When the two friends drove away from the animal hospital fifteen minutes later, Jordan filled Megan in on all the details.

"How were they able to find you to let you know about Odie?"

Jordan looked over at her friend. "I had a microchip put in him a year ago after he went missing for two days. Remember?"

Megan nodded. "Oh, that's right."

"I need to stop by Peterson's so I can get the delivery van."

"Are you sure you're okay to drive?"

"I'll be fine. I'm just tired. Besides, how will I get to work in the morning, pick up Odie and make my deliveries if I leave my van at the garage?"

"I could drive you," Megan volunteered. "I don't mind."

"That's sweet of you. But I just want to get all the vehicles where they need to be so I can go home and go to bed."

"Will you call me when you get home?"

Megan was her best friend and Jordan knew she was just concerned about her. She chuckled. "Yes, Mother."

When they arrived at Peterson's, Jordan went to find Jimmy. "I'm so sorry for yelling at you this afternoon." Then she explained to him what had happened.

The mechanic sympathized with her. "Don't worry about it. I have two black labs at home and I know how it feels when something like that happens."

After she paid the bill for the van, she thanked him for being so understanding.

When Jordan pulled into her driveway, it didn't take her long to discover how Odie had gotten out. She noticed the back gate was standing open. The utility companies didn't need to go back there to read any of the meters, so she was puzzled as to how that could've happened. On her way to investigate, she noticed some broken branches on a couple of the rose bushes next to the house.

She took a minute to scan the yard. That's when she saw that the shed door was ajar. Cold fingers of panic squeezed around her heart when she entered her backyard. She froze. *Who would do this? Was the intruder still around? Did they break into the house?* Her pulse was pounding as she reached into her purse for her cell phone. She dialed 911, told the dispatcher what had happened, and gave her the address. Jordan waited out by her car until the police arrived. She felt angry and scared.

It was Officer Davis. "Hi Brian."

The two had dated for a short time a couple of years ago. But they'd remained friends. She hadn't seen him for several months and had forgotten just how good-looking he was. She caught the familiar scent of the manly aftershave he'd always worn. It caused a flutter in the pit of her stomach. After all this time, her body's reaction to him caught her off guard. Jordan's thoughts drifted back in time, reminiscing about the wonderful few months they'd shared together. Brian had been a pleasant exception to her "all-handsome-guys-are-scum" theory. He was a sweet and thoughtful man. It was sad that things hadn't worked out between them. She'd been ready to settle down, but he'd wanted to focus on his career. A part of her wondered if he'd ever regretted that decision.

"How've you been, Jordan?"

She shook her head before relaying the details of her stress-filled afternoon. "I've had better days."

"I'm sorry about Odie. I hope he's going to be okay." His smooth, rich voice washed over her, and she was glad he'd been the one on duty tonight.

"Thanks." She managed a smile, gazing up into his hazel eyes.

Jordan asked about his folks, and he asked about Andy. A few minutes later, Brian glanced at this watch. "I better get started on my report." Taking out his note pad, he asked her several questions before heading into the backyard to look around.

She followed him as he studied the ground near the shed. Moving closer, she poked her head inside. At first glance, it didn't appear that anything was missing, but whoever had rummaged through her stuff left a big mess. Some of the crystal floral containers were shattered on the floor while other boxes had been opened and rifled through. The extent of the damage was hard to determine. It was starting to get dark and without a flashlight, she couldn't see much past the first couple of feet. Tomorrow she'd clean up the glass and then take inventory of what was left. While the officer continued to look around the yard, she went back inside the house.

Soon, she heard the kitchen door open. It was Brian.

"I jotted down a few things, but I didn't really find much we can use to figure out who might have done this. There are a couple of unusable shoe prints where the person slipped in the dirt by the gate. Also, I found a little blood on one of your rose bushes. I clipped part of the branch. I'll take it in and have it tested to see if we get a hit in the system."

Jordan listened closely to what he was telling her. It sounded like it was pretty hopeless that they'd find out who did this. "So now what?"

"You should call your insurance company

in the morning and file a claim for the damages. I'll make sure the report is ready for you to fax to them. I'll also contact your neighbors to see if they heard or saw anything. Until I have more information, my suggestion would be to install a heavy duty lock lower down on the inside of the gate," Brian said, motioning with his hand. "That way someone can't easily reach over and open it. Plus, you should reinforce the wooden supports and the fence around it. They're a little rickety. As far as the shed goes, you'll want to put a sturdy padlock on the doors. At least then, if someone tries to break in, they'd have to pry the brackets off—or bring bolt cutters with them." He sighed softly. "I noticed the hinges on the door look like they got tweaked and will need to be repaired. I'm sure whoever built it for you could fix the damage without any trouble."

Another man's handsome face appeared in Jordan's mind. *No, that's not an option.* "Thanks, Brian. I'll get those locks replaced and the repairs done as soon as I can. I appreciate you coming over." Standing on her tiptoes, she wrapped her arms around the neck of an old friend and gave him a quick hug.

"That's my job, Jordan." He smiled. "It

was good to see you again. Take care."

After Brian left, Luke's image stayed fixed in her mind. She was grateful he'd been there when she'd needed him this afternoon. He'd been kind and supportive, offering his help without hesitation—in spite of how rude she'd been to him at Peterson's. But still, Jordan hated the fact that she'd had to rely on him today. She also hated the way she'd allowed Luke to comfort her at the vet's office and how her body had felt pressed against his. Tingling sensations raced through her at the memory of his tender embrace.

She was so drained after all the emotional turmoil she'd had to deal with today, the only thing she wanted to do was get cleaned up and crawl under the covers. She felt some of her anxiety dissolve as the water cascaded across her skin.

Twenty minutes later, she'd locked up the house and was finally able to go to bed. Even though she was exhausted, her brain wouldn't shut down. Luke's sexy smile and twinkling eyes appeared every time she was about to drift off. Jordan wished things could be different between them, but that was impossible. As much as she was reluctant to admit it, she still loved him—and probably always would.

But acknowledging those feelings didn't change the harsh reality that he'd deceived her and planned to humiliate her. No matter how good it felt to be back in his arms again, she needed to focus. The most important thing now was to get Odie home and take care of him. Dwelling on what might have been was a waste of time.

It was over.

It had to be.

After Luke left the vet's office, he couldn't stop thinking about Jordan and Odie. He was glad that he had been able to help her. He almost drove over to her house to check things out, but she'd been adamant that she didn't want any further help from him. He had hoped that the next time he saw her, they could discuss the night she'd found the journal. But today hadn't been the right time to bring it up. Later in bed, he thought about how amazing it had been to hold her again, if only for a few minutes. He missed her. *Maybe after Odie gets better, she'll give me another chance to explain. I need her to believe that I'd never hurt her.*

Chapter 15

In a seedy motel on the outskirts of town, a dingy room reeked of cigarettes, mold, and cheap alcohol. The faint smell of a rose scented air freshener lingered in the background. No doubt an attempt by the housekeeper to mask the unpleasant odors imbedded in the thread-bare carpet and pale yellow walls.

A balding man in his fifty's stood in the tiny, mildew-covered bathroom pouring anti-septic over the cuts and scratches on his arms and hands. "Ouch!" He flinched, stretching a Band-Aid across the deepest wound. "This is all that fleabag's fault! If she'd kept him locked up, none of this would've happened!"

He'd wanted to go inside the house and look for valuables, especially after the items in the shed had proven to be worthless. Half way to the back steps, a wild animal had come flying out of the plastic doggie door and chased after him. The snarling lump of tan and white fur followed him through the gate. When the man had made the unfortunate mistake of glancing back over his shoulder, the pooch had nipped at the hem of his pants. With a few vigorous shakes of his leg, the aggressive mutt went tumbling across the grass. The man scowled at all the red marks on his tanned skin. *That's when I stumbled into one of those damned rose bushes next to the house. And while "Fido" was still rolling on the ground, I had just enough time to make it to the car.*

Before packing up the first aid supplies, he treated one more painful spot from his adventure this afternoon. Yanking out part of a thorn jammed into his wrist, the man grimaced again, shaking his hand back and forth until the sting subsided.

The dog had guts though, he'd give him that. Still, he hadn't meant to hit him. He'd just wanted to scare him a little when he'd swerved the car. *How was I supposed to know the mongrel was too stupid to get out of the way?* At least none of her nosey neighbors had witnessed what had happened. He'd made sure of that. The man had been casing the block for almost a week; different times of day, different hidden locations. There weren't many houses on that street. Besides, those old fools were creatures of habit. They left the same time every day for work and who knows where.

When he finished taking care of his injuries, he studied the city street map laying on top of the stained, lime-green and orange flowered bedspread. *I have to be more careful next time. I can't blow it now.* Knowing he'd have to change his plans, he let out a heavy breath. Breaking into her business was just too risky. The surrounding area was well lit and the cops patrolled the parking lot on a regular basis. He squinted and stared at the wall, trying to remember if he'd seen a security alarm key pad inside the shop. Chuckling to himself, he recalled the day he'd watched the owner leave before strolling in, pretending to be legitimate customer. That little twit she had working there left him alone for a few minutes, which gave him the opportunity he needed to scan the layout. He was even able to sneak a peek at the workroom, locating the office and back door. *She wouldn't have much money lying around anyway.* Every afternoon he'd watched as one of the women walked to the bank and made a deposit. There was probably a small safe located somewhere inside, but he doubted there was enough money in it to make it worth taking such a chance. *Besides, all that was in there was flowery junk,* he thought shaking his head in disgust. He'd seen some activity out by the old house. Maybe he'd go check it out tomorrow.

Tipping his head back, he downed the last of the bourbon then tossed the bottle in the trash can with a clank. There was a bar next door and, at this hour, he shouldn't have any trouble finding a willing woman to keep him company—at least for a few hours. He'd charm her into believing she'd hit the jackpot and found Mr. Wonderful. When in reality, she'd be just a throw-away good time to help relieve some of his stress.

The man examined his hazy image in the bathroom mirror under two bare bulbs—one burned out. The cover had long ago been removed or broken, he guessed, by the amount of dust perched atop them like snow piled on the roof of an abandoned car after a bad storm. The mirror's reflective film had clouded, and flecks had peeled away from the edges over time. His cold, dark eyes saw only what he wanted to see—the face of a much younger man. A face that once held promises for a happy future, full of hopes and dreams. A face minus the deep creases, evidence of a life lived hard and reckless. No receding hairline, no dark circles under the now-vacant eyes.

He turned the squeaky knob and water stuttered out of the faucet, splattering all around him. A rust-colored trail started underneath the worn silver fixture, cascaded down the inside of the chipped, porcelain sink, and disappeared into the drain. It matched the one in the grimy tub behind him. After a few swipes of his comb through the mostly clear water, he slicked down his hair before splashing on too much cheap cologne.

Standing next to the bed, he threw on a pair of jeans, leather boots, and a white shirt; intentionally leaving the top three buttons unfastened. He slipped his arms into a worn, dark green, sport coat then took another quick glance in the mirror. The man tossed an approving wink at the reflection staring back at him.

It was time to go. "Get ready, ladies. One of you is about to get lucky and experience the best night of sex you've ever had." An evil laugh followed him out into the darkness as he closed the motel door behind him.

❀ ❀ ❀

On Friday, the shop had been busy with customers and Jordan was thankful for the distractions. She'd explained to Darcy what had happened. The girl said how sorry she was that Odie had been hurt. Jordan made a few phone calls to arrange for a handyman friend of hers to install the new lock on the gate and reinforce the posts. She didn't have time to worry about the shed today. She'd cleaned up the broken glass before going to work, but she'd wait to take a better look inside this weekend.

Dr. Leonard called about two o'clock and told Jordan that Odie's tests were normal. "He's a lucky boy. We didn't find anything else wrong with him other than a few bruises and a scrape or two. You can pick him up any time after four this afternoon. All the girls here have fallen in love with him and they're going to miss him. He's quite the little character."

"Yeah, he is," Jordan said with a chuckle. "See you later."

The next couple of hours seemed to drag on and on. Finally, three forty-five. She was so excited she could hardly wait to pick him up. She left Darcy in charge of the shop for the rest of the day and rushed out the door with instructions to call her cell phone if there was an emergency.

Driving faster than she should have, Jordan made it to the vet's office in record time. Walking up to the reception desk, she greeted Jill, the same girl she'd spoken to yesterday. "Hi, I'm here to pick up my dog. His name's Odie."

"Let me find his file, Ms. Shaw and I'll be right back with you."

Jordan took out her credit card, tapping it against the counter while she waited. This was going to put a big dent in her savings. When the girl returned, Jordan asked, "How much do I owe you?"

Jill closed the file and smiled up at Jordan. "You're good to go, Ms. Shaw. The file shows a zero balance due."

Jordan stared at her. "You must be mistaken. I haven't paid anything yet."

"No. I'm positive. The bill has been taken care of," the girl assured her.

"I don't understand. Maybe it's for another dog. Odie's a little brown and white terrier mix, about this big." She motioned with her hands. "He came in yesterday with a broken leg." Jordan was puzzled and asked Jill to please check again.

The young girl sighed and opened the file. She picked up the phone and paged someone in the back. Jordan heard her ask if there had been any other dog treated in the last couple of days with that description or that name. After hanging up, she looked up at Jordan. "No, Ms. Shaw, he's the only dog by that name and description that we have." She flipped the file open once more and lifted the top page. "It's right here." Jill pointed at a spot on the paper. "Paid in full this morning by a Mr. Luke Kincaid."

Shocked by what she'd heard, Jordan's mouth dropped open. "What? But..." She stared at Jill.

"Ms. Shaw, please have a seat. Someone will bring your dog out shortly."

Jordan nodded. A couple of minutes later, she heard a familiar bark. Dr. Leonard appeared around the corner carrying a squirming Odie. He almost jumped out of the vet's arms he was so happy to see his owner. Once she wrapped her arms around him, she placed a kiss on the top of his furry head.

He wiggled every which way in order to lick her face as his tail thumped enthusiastically against her side. Dr. Leonard handed Jordan a small bottle of pain pills for Odie with instructions to give him one in the morning and one at dinnertime. The vet suggested she try hiding them in a piece of cheese or wrapped in slice of his favorite lunchmeat.

Jordan cuddled her dog close as tears formed in her eyes. "Thank you so much for taking such good care of him."

"You're welcome. Try to keep him inside as much as possible, I don't want him running and jumping around on that leg," Dr. Leonard warned. "You'll also have to put him on a leash when you take him outside, that way you can control his rambunctious energy." The vet smiled as she ruffled the fur on Odie's head. "Now, I need to see him back here in six weeks so I can examine him to see if his cast can come off."

Out in the parking lot, Jordan carefully placed Odie in his carrier for the trip home. He didn't really like being in there, but she knew it would be much safer than letting him stumble around in a moving car.

After arriving home, she noticed it was a real struggle for the dog to move around. He'd look down at the foreign object on his leg and then focus those big, brown eyes up at her. Talking softly, she tried to reassure him with the tone of her voice that everything would be okay. Odie tried to walk, but he'd whine every time his little blue leg slipped on the hardwood floor. Jordan found a small, round rubber stopper like you'd use on the bottom of a chair leg. There was a strong adhesive backing, so she pressed it onto the end of the cast. That seemed to solve the problem.

She fed him, gave him his pill and took him outside. Later, she eased Odie onto his favorite blanket next to her on the couch. Stroking his fur, she noticed it didn't take long before he was sound asleep. She finished watching a movie on TV then gently carried him to bed. He snuggled against her. She hoped she'd wake up if he stirred or needed to go outside in the middle of the night. She didn't want her little, wounded guy jumping off the bed, but she didn't have the heart to make him stay in his crate all night.

Even though she was overjoyed and grateful that Odie hadn't been injured any worse, her heart still broke for him. He whimpered in his sleep a couple of times and then seemed to settle down. It took a while before Jordan felt comfortable enough to close her eyes, allowing herself to drift off.

Driving down the two-lane road on Friday, a couple of hours before dusk, the foremost thought in the devious man's mind was to confirm that nobody had moved into the old house. In order for him to successfully execute his plan, he couldn't be found snooping around the place. A few minutes later, he shrewdly stashed the Buick in a deserted barn on an adjacent section of property.

A grove of trees bordering the backyard of his former home was all that stood between him and the extravagant destiny he was absolutely certain he was entitled to. Maneuvering his way across the thick, autumn carpet scattered with twigs and leaves, he paused every few feet to survey the area around him. After a moment or two he continued on. Step by step, he threaded himself through the jumbled maze of pines and the now barren, brown and gray limbs of the other trees and shrubs.

An unmistakable, earthy smell surrounded him. It mingled with the pungent scents of evergreens and a spiciness from the damp, decaying ground cover closest to the soil. He took a deep breath.

His senses sparked with awareness, forcing him to remember the last day he'd walked these woods.

A lot of years had passed since he'd been back here. Most everything looked eerily unchanged, as if time had stood still. The buildings appeared to have been neglected and unoccupied for quite a while. They could definitely use a fresh coat of paint. Weeds had claimed the space where there had once been a thick, green lawn with a vegetable garden in the corner underneath the kitchen window.

Dressed in tan pants and jacket, the man blended in with his surrounding while he lurked in a dense patch of bushes at the edge of the yard. About forty-five minutes had gone by, but he remained hidden, keeping an eye out for anyone who might be nearby. The temperature was starting to drop. His legs were aching from crouching in one position for so long. "I'm getting too old for this crap," he groused, rubbing his throbbing knees as he stood. *It's a good thing I'll be back in the sunshine in a couple of weeks; this time for good. And then I'll never have to set foot in this God-forsaken town again.*

Just when the man thought it was safe enough to emerge from his hiding place and wander into the backyard, a green pickup turned down the gravel road heading in his direction. He quickly ducked back down out of sight. "Who is *this* guy?" he muttered under his breath.

Luke backed his truck up along the side of the building. It made carrying what he'd need for his next few projects easier. Propping open the back door of the house, he started to unload the equipment. He took a moment to take in what he'd accomplished so far. All of his hard work was paying off and it looked even better than he'd originally imagined.

The man's eyes squinted beneath overgrown brows. It was getting more difficult to see because daylight was fading quickly. Concealed in the shadows, he watched the younger man make several trips back and forth from the vehicle. The sign on the driver's door read Kincaid Construction. *I wonder if he's fixing the house up for someone else or for him.* He grinned maliciously. *This is an intriguing and unexpected turn of events.* From what the man could see, the tools looked expensive. Dollars signs flashed in his brain as each item was removed from the truck and hauled inside. There was a guy across the state line, that he still kept in contact with, who'd give him top dollar for the stuff—in cash, without questioning how he'd acquired them. After waiting for another half an hour, he realized the man inside the house didn't plan on leaving soon enough to satisfy him. He'd have to come back another time. Knowing sound carries more at night, the man carefully inched his way in the direction of the barn.

Before exiting the woods, he stopped and listened for any movement around the dilapidated wooden structure. He crept inside, got into the car, and turned the key in the ignition, and eased the Buick out into the open and down the dirt road. Leaning his left elbow on the small arm rest attached to the door, he let his finger slowly drift across the dark stubble on his chin. The appearance of the guy at the old house forced him to rethink his current plan. Deep in thought all the way back to town, his brain struggled to devise a new one.

He stopped and bought a six-pack of beer, made a quick swing through a McDonald's, then drove to the run-down motel. Back in his room, he processed the information he'd gathered tonight. "I sure would like to know what that guy is doing out at the old house," he mumbled to the man in the bathroom mirror. The question would have to go unanswered. It wasn't like he could just stroll into the courthouse and inquire about the deed. Frank still worked there. He'd seen him go inside the historical brick building early in the morning one day and leave later that afternoon. So that wasn't an option. He didn't have a computer, and the library was off limits, too. That old biddy, Mrs. Henson, would recognize him for sure, even after all this time. Some people in this town would never forget his face—or what he'd done.

After thinking about it a little more, he decided it didn't really matter as long as he could retrieve what was his and not get caught. As soon as his mission was completed, he wouldn't waste a second getting out of town.

He lay down on the bed to watch some old movie, but started to yawn after only twenty minutes. Between the greasy burger and fries and the alcohol, he couldn't keep his eyes open any longer. He hadn't gotten much sleep last night either thanks to the busty woman he'd picked up at the bar and brought back to his room. She'd been full of energy and wasn't quite as drunk as he'd thought. *She was a wild one all right.* He shook his head

chuckling wickedly to himself. He'd gotten
what he was after, and then some. He'd allowed her curvaceous body to satisfy him
more than once before sending the feisty red-
head off in a cab at four this morning. Although she'd pleaded to stay, she was no
longer needed. She'd served her purpose.
Stopping by the motel office earlier in the
day, he'd made up some lie about a spring on
the bed poking him in the back. It was necessary that he move to a different room, just in
case she came looking for him. Even though
he'd given her a fake name, he wasn't about
to take any chances.

He was too close to having it all.

And nothing was going to stand in his
way.

The following morning Jordan took Odie
out in the backyard. He appeared to be getting
the hang of his cast. As they walked by the
shed, she recalled what Brian had told her.
*'I'm sure whoever built it for you could fix
the damage without any trouble.'* The more
she thought about it, the more a disturbing
idea invaded Jordan's mind. What if Luke

had been so helpful and kind just to get back in her good graces? Was he trying to soften her heart in hopes that she'd forgive him? Was he taking advantage of this stressful time when she'd been so vulnerable and upset over her poor little dog? Could he be that cold and devious? He'd seemed genuinely worried about Odie at the time.

Then she remembered her conversation with the young woman behind the counter at the vet's office yesterday. '...*Paid in full by a Mr. Luke Kincaid...*' Jill had informed her. Anger rose up in her the more she thought about the events of the last couple of days. Jordan doubted that his motives were as honorable as he wanted her to believe.

The phone at the flower shop rang Monday afternoon. "The Petal Pusher. May I help you?"

"Hello, Jordan." Luke wasn't sure what kind of reception he was going to receive from her. But he was concerned about her—and the dog.

"Luke." Her icy tone answered his question.

"I wanted to check and find out how Odie's doing."

She closed her eyes and leaned her back

against the cool wall next to the display case. "Thank you for paying the vet bill. I intend to reimburse you every cent."

"That's not why I'm calling, and I won't take your money," he said, his voice soft and compassionate. "I was happy to do it. I've been worried about you. I know how much you love that little guy."

Jordan took a deep breath. Why did he have to talk to her that way? And why did his deep voice send her pulse into overdrive no matter how mad she was at him? "I insist on repaying the debt." Her determined attitude came through loud and clear. "Like I told you the other day, Mr. Kincaid, I appreciated your help, but the health of my dog is none of your business. And, neither is how *I'm* doing."

Hanging up the phone, she felt a twinge of regret at the way she'd spoken to Luke. She probably shouldn't have been so rude. Maybe in a couple of days, she'd call and apologize to him. It was just so stressful dealing with her unwanted feelings towards him, especially now while Odie was sick. She squeezed her eyes tight, trying to think. How was she going to figure out if Luke was being sincere or if he had ulterior motives, playing her for a fool—again?

Chapter 16

A couple weeks before Thanksgiving, Jordan was busy working at the flower shop. She'd just finished her last arrangement for the day and was placing it in the cooler, when the phone rang. "Good afternoon, The Petal Pusher, may I help you?"

"Hey, Sis." Andy's voice sounded hesitant and lacked some of its familiar cheerfulness. That was a sure sign that he had something to tell her—something he didn't really want to.

"What's up, little brother?"

He paused then stammered. "I—uh—I can't make it for Thanksgiving." His rehearsed explanation poured out of his mouth. "I have a chance to take a high powered hotshot from L.A. and a few of his colleagues on one of those week long extreme adventure trips. It would be great for business. It's a once in a lifetime opportunity and could open a lot of doors for me, otherwise you know I'd be there. You understand, right?"

Jordan was silent. She couldn't believe that her only family was bailing on her. Closing her eyes, she rubbed her forehead. This would mean she'd spend the entire day alone.

His guilty conscience convinced him that her silence meant only one thing. "Come on, M.J., don't be mad. I promise I'll make it up to you at Christmas. I'll buy you an extra great present. I'll even take you out to dinner, my treat. I'll shovel the snow outside your store and your house. I'll—" The sound of regret filled his voice more and more with each passing second.

"Andy—Andy, it's fine, I understand. I'm proud of you and I'm glad your business is doing so well. You need to take the job. I'll be fine." She tried to sound supportive because she knew that making her brother feel bad wouldn't do either of them any good.

"Are you sure? I can call Craig and have him take them out instead, if you really want me to."

"No, you go do what you need to and don't worry about me, I'll be fine. Maybe I'll even take the weekend off and head to a spa to get away before the Christmas rush." Jordan knew she wouldn't, but it was better than telling Andy she'd sit at home alone, probably crying in her frozen turkey dinner. She still battled with the heartache from her fight with Luke, and there hadn't been a day since then she hadn't cried. Even though he'd plotted to expose her family's secret, she still loved him and missed him very much.

She could always volunteer at the community center and help serve meals to the homeless. Doing something good for others would hopefully take her mind off Luke and put her problems into perspective. Besides, she didn't have the energy for an all-day pity party where she was the only guest.

"Thanks, Sis. I really appreciate it. I'll call you when I get back and tell you how the trip went." Andy's voice sounded like the little boy she remembered growing up, especially after he'd charmed their mother into getting his way.

"I'll be looking forward to it. Have a good time." Jordan tried to sound happy for him and deep down in her heart she truly was.

The next couple of days were steady at the flower shop with customers ordering centerpieces of orange, yellow and rust colored flowers for their holiday tables. Each order made her feel more and more sad and lonely. She called to find out the times and locations of the missions, churches, and shelters where her help was needed.

Luke leaned his shoulder against one of the support beams on the back porch of the old house while nursing a cup of coffee. The early morning air was crisp and wisps of steam rose from his mug like tiny anorexic ghosts. A hawk soared in the gray sky, dipping and floating on the currents. As he stared at the grove of trees in front of him, he noticed patches of green from the pines showing through the tangled mass of barren branches. It was the only color in the surrounding landscape this time of year.

So many things had changed over the last few months. Behind him stood the house that had not only transformed in appearance, but also in what it represented. It had started out as a business investment, but it quickly turned into an emotional one. It had been difficult to work here these last few weeks. He couldn't shake the images of Jordan from his thoughts. The way she looked and how she felt nestled up against him that morning on her couch. The way her lips were soft and warm on his when they kissed. But the memory of the hurt he'd witnessed on her face, that night she'd accused him of betraying her, overshadowed them all and was foremost in his mind.

If he couldn't convince Jordan that she was wrong about his intentions—an icy fear rushed through him. Closing his eyes, Luke willed himself to concentrate. He had to think of a way to get Jordan to listen to him.

The plans for the house had been modified after he'd fallen in love with her. It really wasn't set up to be a bed and breakfast anymore, should the worst case scenario play out. The possibility of that happening produced a stabbing pain in the middle of his chest. Luke's coffee had grown cold, so he tossed the remainder over the wooden railing and went back inside.

Refinishing the wood floors, moldings, and staircase banister were the items next on the agenda. It would take a lot of muscle and tedious work, but the finished product was going to be well worth it. The deep, rich honeys and browns would bring warmth and hominess to the rooms.

Luke had tried to call Jordan again, but she refused to speak to him and hung up, not even giving him a chance to say anything. He was out of ideas, but he couldn't give up. He loved her and wanted her back in his life. There had to be a way to convince her, to make her understand.

It was finally Saturday and Jordan was done working for the week. She stopped by the grocery store on her way home to pick up a few things. As she stared into the meat case, Sam, the butcher, walked out from the back wiping his hands on his bloodstained apron.

"Hi, Jordan. Can I help you with anything? The sirloins are on sale today and they're top quality."

She hated shopping for just one person, but peering through the glass at the steaks, she decided to take a couple. "Okay, I'll take two. Can you wrap them separately please? I'll freeze one for later."

"Sure thing. Anything else I can get for you today?"

"Would you happen to have any bones back there for Odie?" She arched her eyebrows and accompanied her request with an impish smile.

He gave her a friendly nod. "I'm sure I can find some. How's his leg doing?"

"Thanks to Dr. Leonard, he's as feisty as ever."

In a few minutes, Sam returned with her steaks and two extra packages wrapped in brown butcher paper. "Here you go, Jordan. The bones are on the house."

"Thanks Sam, I appreciate it. I know he'll love them." She continued her shopping, pushing her cart up and down each aisle, randomly tossing in items, most of which she didn't really need.

At home, Odie greeted her at the door with a mixture of barks and whines, adding a couple of spins for good measure. His furry, white tail wagged so hard he almost tipped over.

"I've got a surprise for you," Jordan announced looking into his big brown eyes. The dog's ears pricked up and he sat down as if he knew something special was about to happen. The minute she unwrapped one of the bones, his whole body started to tremble with anticipation and excitement. "Here you go, boy."

Eager to enjoy his unexpected present, Odie gently took the bone from her fingers. He scampered through the doggie door and out into the backyard as the plastic flap clattered behind him. Jordan had to chuckle to herself at how such a small thing could make him so happy.

Even though he could be a stinker at times, she didn't know what she'd do without him. The love she received from that fuzzy little guy was deep and unconditional. He didn't care about her past or what her bank account said. He just wanted to snuggle up next to her on the couch or crawl under the covers of her bed at night.

While she put away the groceries, thoughts of Luke wrapped around her heart. God, how she missed him. And how she still loved him. A love that wouldn't die quickly or painlessly. If only he hadn't found her journal and schemed to betray her like that. If her past could be different, if only—but it couldn't, and there was nothing she could do to change it.

Later, while curled up on the sofa under her favorite afghan, she looked forward to watching her sit-coms on television. They made her laugh and helped her get lost for a little while, away from the reality of her life.

Luke kept replaying the confrontation with Jordan that night at his house over and over in his mind. What could he have said differently to convince her that his love was real? That her family and her past didn't matter to him? Frustration was building up inside of him as he roamed in and out of his bedroom one night, eventually igniting a wave of anger. "Why won't she listen to me or let me explain? How can she say it's over between us until she knows the whole story?" Luke sat down on the edge of the bed with his head in his hands. "Over?" The word traveled on a loud exhale out into the dark room. He bolted off the bed, "The hell it is! It's not over for me by a long shot!" In the next instant, snatching up one of his work boots, he flung it across the room.

He was determined to give it one more try. He didn't have time to rehearse what he was going to say, he just pointed his truck in the direction of Jordan's house. With his stomach in knots, he pulled into her driveway, took a deep breath, and rang the doorbell.

The sudden noise startled Jordan. She couldn't imagine who would be dropping by her house on a Saturday night. When she opened the door, her heart started pounding in her chest, reacting immediately to the handsome face staring back at her.

"Hello, Jordan." His eyes searched her

face for any kind of sign that her attitude had
softened toward him.

At first, she was excited to see him. But in
a matter of seconds, the painful memory of
what he'd done re-opened the wound that had
barely started to heal. "What are you doing
here, Luke?" She crossed her arms defensively over her chest, like a shield, somehow believing it would protect what was left of her
heart against any further damage from the
man who had turned her world upside down.
"I told you I didn't want to see you again."
She tried to be strong, unwilling to let him
discover how much she still loved him, but
seeing him standing there just inches away,
made her voice tremble. "Now please, just go
away." She started to close the door, but Luke
stuck his heavy, steel-toed work boot in the
opening to block it.

"No, Jordan. I won't leave until you hear
me out." His pulse was racing, but he was determined to make her listen to his side of the
story.

"There's nothing left to say." Unshed tears
burned in her eyes, as she hid behind the solid
oak door, leaning her forehead against it. She
refused to let him see how vulnerable she was
around him.

"I disagree, my love, there's a lot I have to say."

She wished he wouldn't call her that, not now, when she was trying so hard to resist him. Jordan's willpower was fading with every moment he stood there. She wanted to fling the door open and rush into his arms, but she couldn't. Steeling herself the best she could, she finally relented and opened the door to face him. "If I let you say whatever it is that you think is so important, will you leave me alone and not come back?" Her eyes pleaded with him.

"I can't make you that promise, Jordan," he responded with a gentle, but matter-of-fact tone.

Releasing a sigh of defeat, she waved him inside. She took a seat on the far end of the couch, pulled her knees up to her chest, and wrapped the afghan tight around her.

Luke stood across the room gathering his thoughts. "Jordan, I'm sorry I didn't give you the journal when I realized it was yours. But it wasn't because I was going to use it against you. I was trying to think of the best way to let you know that I'd found it and, ah—that I'd read it. I was afraid of how you'd react. I didn't want to lose you. I love you."

"You played me for fool. And now I'm supposed to believe that you did it because you didn't know how to tell me you knew about my past?" Anger and hurt welled up inside her. She didn't want to hear his lame excuses again.

"It's the truth, Jordan. I was going to show you the journal that night, but you found it before I had a chance to explain."

"Explain? Maybe you should explain the conversation I overheard about how you had a great idea that would make a lot of money and how you couldn't wait to get out of here."

Luke wished he knew the right words to say to make her understand. "It's not what you think. You only heard parts of that conversation."

Her eyes narrowed. "You and your friend were going to sell my journal and humiliate me. Don't try to deny it." Hot tears began to roll down her cheeks. "I've worked very hard to put my past behind me and start over, but you were going to ruin it all. Now you have the nerve to stand here and tell me that you love me? Well, Mr. Kincaid, how much did you expect to get paid to buy your proclamation of undying love for me?" She threw back the afghan and jumped to her feet, spearing the air between them with her index finger. "I hope it was worth it!"

Odie had been sitting a few feet away listening, but when Jordan suddenly stood and confronted Luke, the little dog moved closer to his owner, his protection mode on full alert.

"If you'd listen to me for a second, I'm trying to explain that you misunderstood—"

"I'm not an idiot, Luke, so don't treat me like one. I know what I heard!" She threw her hands up, her eyes flaming with bitterness and resentment.

A low growl filled the air between them. When Jordan looked down she realized that Odie was ready to defend her. "Stop it!" He obeyed, but his black eyes stayed fixed on the man in front of him.

"Jordan, I was talking about selling *my* house, not your journal. You didn't hear the whole conversation." His eyes begged her to believe him. "I do love you and I would never do anything like that to you. You have to believe me."

"I don't have to believe anything you say. Love can always be bought for the right price! My daddy's love for my mother was purchased with the body of a younger woman and stolen money. Brad's love was purchased by selfish pride. Greg's promise of love was just a ploy to have one more fling before he got married. So don't expect me to become a naïve, twittering schoolgirl just because you say you're sorry while standing here declaring your love for me." Jordan's voice trembled, but her tone was undeniably bitter. Cold, hard eyes glared at him from behind pools of unshed tears.

Walking over to the chair where his jacket was draped across the seat, Luke reached under it and pulled out a flat box wrapped in gold foil paper. He held it out to her, "Here, open it, then maybe you'll believe me."

"Whatever it is, I don't want it. Now, will you please leave?" Jordan walked in the direction of the door, but Luke stepped in front of her, blocking her path.

"Not until you open this," he insisted.

"Has anyone ever told you how bullheaded and exasperating you are?"

"Once or twice." He slid a cocky grin in place as she reached for the box.

"Fine, if I open this," she snapped, waving the package at him, "then will you leave?"

"If that's what you really want, Jordan."

The muscle along his jaw twitched when he answered.

"Fine, get your keys out of your pocket," she urged, ripping at the paper. "Because you'll be leaving in a—" She stopped when she discovered what was inside. With a startled gasp, she blinked a couple of times to make sure she wasn't seeing things. Almost afraid to touch it, Jordan carefully removed the beautiful leather book. She glanced up at Luke and then back down to a cherished piece of her past. Gently, she opened the cover and tears stared to fall when she recognized the handwriting from a lifetime ago. "My journal," she whispered, her tone part statement, part question.

Watching her fingers trace page after page of memories, Luke took a step closer. "The conversation you heard was with my friend, Mike. He repairs old books. You heard only bits and pieces of our discussion. I was telling him about the woman I loved and how I wanted to surprise her by restoring her journal. But then, when you flung it at my head that night, pages fell out and the binding was damaged, so he had to do a little more work on it than originally planned." Luke pulled a yellow paper out of the back pocket of his jeans and showed it to Jordan. It was the receipt for repairing her journal.

Embarrassed, heat colored her cheeks as she gazed up at Luke. "I don't know what to say. I—I said such horrible—"

"You don't have to say anything. The expression on your face tells me all I need to know. So now do you believe that I wasn't scheming against you?"

Fresh tears were his answer. Lines formed on Jordan's forehead. "But I heard you talk about extra money and leaving. I don't understand."

"The extra money is from a large new project that my company was hired to do. I'm not putting my house on the market for a few months, but I have plans to move into another home before long. Hopefully." A picture appeared in his mind of the old house and Jordan, a yard with a couple of kids, and even Odie. "I have the paperwork for that, too, if you want to see it."

"No, that's okay. I believe you," she responded softly with a shake of her head,

Luke pulled her to him. "I love you, Jordan. I don't want you to ever doubt that. I fell in love with you as the young woman, M.J., but I love you so much more as the beautiful person you are now. I'm not your father, or Brad, or Greg. I won't ever hurt you like that, I promise."

They stood together, arms wrapped tightly around each other for several minutes. A contented silence filled the room, neither one speaking nor expecting the other one to. They just *were*—and it felt like home.

Chapter 17

When Luke and Jordan entered the house, wonderful smells of the holiday greeted them: roast turkey, baked ham, plus nutmeg and cinnamon from the homemade apple and pumpkin pies.

"Mother?" he called.

"In here," came a voice from the kitchen.

Making their way in that direction, they found Anna busy stacking plates and counting out silverware. A pair of gray-haired ladies bustled around the room stirring pots of this and checking on covered dishes of that. Luke recognized them as the Clark sisters who lived two houses down. They were friends of his mother and about her age. Neither of them had ever married and they didn't have any relatives left around Hilldale. Even though there were only going to be five for dinner, Anna asked them to help her. It wasn't often that her family was all together. The sisters loved to cook, so it was a win-win situation. They made a little extra money doing something they enjoyed. Anna was free to spend some quality time with her beloved sons and daughter-in-law. Besides, after talking to Luke, Anna's motherly intuition told her that Jordan might become a part of their little group before long.

Luke kissed his mom on the cheek. Anna hugged her son and then Jordan. "I'm so happy you could join us."

"Thank you for inviting me, especially on such short notice." A hint of color invaded Jordan's face as she thought about the recent situation between her and Luke. "Can I help you with anything?"

"Heavens no, you're our guest." Anna waved her off. "Son, why don't the two of you go into the family room, nibble on a few snacks, and get comfortable. Philip and Audra should be here any minute and I'll be in shortly." As they walked down the hall, they couldn't help but snicker when they overheard Anna giving instructions. "Doris, I think the mashed potatoes need a little more salt. Mary, don't let the vegetables get overcooked now."

Luke and Jordan sampled just enough of the delicious finger foods to satisfy their rumbling stomachs before settling down on the comfy couch. The Macy's parade was on TV and they began sharing childhood memories of watching it as kids. About twenty minutes later, familiar voices could be heard in the other room. The last two members of the family had arrived.

Philip was the first to make an appearance, slapping Luke on the arm as he walked by. "What's up big brother? Who's this pretty lady?" A mischievous smile accompanied Philip's teasing. "And how much did you have to pay her to come here with you today?"

"Very funny. For your information, this gorgeous lady is my *girlfriend*, Jordan Shaw."

"So you're the famous Jordan. Nice to meet you." Accepting her hand, Philip kissed the back of her knuckles.

She was happy to play along. "It's a pleasure to finally meet Luke's handsome younger brother."

"And as you can plainly see, *I* am the more attractive one."

Luke huffed. "Please, don't insult her intelligence, Philip. It's obvious to her that *I'm* the more ruggedly handsome one. She's just being polite so you don't get your feelings hurt." The brothers bantered back and forth in boyish sibling rivalry, producing waves of laughter from the trio. Philip nodded toward Luke, conveying a silent communication that he approved of Jordan.

"Where's Audra?" Luke asked.

"She's talking to Mother." Philip turned his attention to Jordan. "I heard you've already met my wife."

"Yes, I have." Pink invaded her cheeks again wondering how much of the story had been relayed to him, probably all of it, judging by the smirk on his face.

"All joking aside, Jordan, I'm glad you could share the day with us." Philip's words seemed genuine and she felt a pang of jealousy at what a wonderful family Luke had. Once upon a time, she'd convinced herself that her family had been ideal, but they never had this much fun together, except maybe when Grams was around. But then after her father...well, things were just never the same. The sound of male laughter carried Jordan back to the present and she could feel the unspoken love between the two men.

"We've got a surprise for you. I'll be right back." Philip exited the room for just a moment. "I hope you're ready to be an uncle, big brother," he announced, right before walking in next to Audra. A noticeable belly bump protruded from under a cream-colored designer shirt. Luke and Jordan took turns congratulating both expectant parents-to-be.

"When are you due?" Jordan asked.

"The middle of February," Audra drawled in her smooth, southern accent, gazing up at her husband who beamed proudly from ear to ear.

"Why didn't you tell me?" Luke asked his brother.

"Well, we wanted to wait until we were sure things checked out okay." Philip paused, wrapping one arm around his wife in a loving and supportive gesture. "You see, we were pregnant last year, but had a miscarriage. We just wanted the doctor to reassure us that the baby's healthy this time before we told anyone."

Luke and Jordan expressed their sympathy for the couple's loss. A few details were exchanged before Philip and Audra steered the conversation back to the topic of the new baby.

"Does Mother know?" Luke questioned his brother.

"We told her a few weeks ago, but since we were coming for Thanksgiving, we asked her to keep it a secret."

"Do you know what you're having?" Jordan asked Audra.

"It's called a baby, Jordan." Elbowing Luke in the ribs, Philip shook his head. "You really need to explain the way the birds and bees work to your girlfriend here." Pointing to Jordan, he flashed her a playful wink. All four laughed at the good-natured teasing.

Audra gently rubbed her hand over her stomach, "No, we want to wait and be surprised."

Just then, Anna joined her family. "*I* hope it's a girl. I raised two boys and I can't wait to buy frilly, lacy little dresses in pink for a granddaughter." Tears of joy formed in the older woman's eyes.

"Well, there was that time we dressed Luke up in Cousin Cindy's pink feety pajamas," Philip reminded her. Another burst of laughter filled the room and Luke shot his brother, a "don't go there" look that was received loud and clear.

"Enough of this, let's go eat." Anna announced, leading the way into the elegantly decorated dining room. Jordan had designed the large floral arrangement that sat in the center of the ivory linen tablecloth. Darcy had delivered it yesterday. Fall flowers in deep, rich shades of reds, yellows, oranges, and burgundy surrounded three rust-colored taper candles. Accents of browns and greens from cattails, twigs, and silk leaves finished off the centerpiece. Everyone complimented Jordan on how beautiful it was. The table looked like a page right out of a Martha Stewart magazine.

"Thank you, but it was my pleasure."

Luke squeezed her hand, silently letting her know that he was glad she was here with him.

Anna tried to coax the sisters into joining them for dinner, but they declined, stating this was a day for family. They preferred to eat in the kitchen together, just the two of them. Their own little family.

Luke and Jordan were on one side, Philip and Audra were on the other, and Anna sat at the head of the table. They all held hands while Anna said grace. A warm sense of belonging spread through Jordan. If it wasn't for the absent father figure, this really would be like a Norman Rockwell painting. They ate, shared stories, and enjoyed each other's company. The meal and the conversation were wonderful.

After the two men went to watch football, the three women chatted about the baby. Anna was excited to start picking out names, clothes, and paint colors for the nursery. Jordan wondered if she and Luke would ever have kids together. The thought startled her since they had barely gotten back together. And even though she loved him, it was way too early to think about babies.

When Anna went to the kitchen to check on her friends, Audra took Jordan's hand in hers and smiled. "It's nice to see you again. I think it's wonderful that you're able to share Thanksgiving with us."

"I feel honored that you all allowed me to be a part of your family celebration. Everyone has been so kind. They've made me feel very welcome."

Audra's smile grew wider. "I'm glad you and Luke were able to resolve that silly little misunderstanding."

Jordan gave her a curious look as anger and fear rose up in her. Luke had apparently shared her family secrets from the journal with *all* the members of his family.

"You thinking I was *Luke's* wife that day

you brought Anna her flowers. I was very emotional and gushing on and on about them. During that time, I was taking hormone shots to help me get pregnant again." She waved her hand in the air. "What a mess, and poor Philip, the things he had to put up with."

Jordan breathed a sigh of relief. But the next heartbeat brought a pang of guilt, pricking her conscience for thinking the comment was about the past she was trying so desperately to hide. This lovely woman had lost a child, and all Jordan could think about was how humiliating it would be if someone found out about her father's indiscretions. Her fear of embarrassment paled in comparison to the pain and suffering Audra had endured.

"I had never met anyone who called their mom by her first name, and then you answered the door. You're so beautiful and you were so excited, plus I noticed that big diamond wedding ring. I just assumed..." Jordan shrugged.

"Well, thank you for the compliment." Audra paused as she thought back to that day. "Now that you've explained it like that, I can see how it would have been confusing."

Jordan offered a small nod. "I appreciate your understanding."

"Luke's a wonderful man. He must think you're very special, otherwise you wouldn't be here today. He's very protective of his family, both the boys are." Silence filled the space between the two women for a few seconds, then Jordan saw a gleam appear in Audra's hazel eyes. "Let's go check on our men," she whispered. "And see if the tryptophan has them snoring yet." The women chuckled softly before making their way down the hall.

Sure enough, the two brothers had fallen asleep, heads tipped back, mouths hanging wide open, oblivious to the football game while the voices of the commentators blared on into the room.

When Luke and Philip woke up from their "nap," they joined the women in the dining room for dessert. Anna eagerly revealed her detailed plans for this year's annual Kincaid Christmas party. Philip and Audra had to fly back home tomorrow, but promised they'd be back for the big celebration.

Anna was delighted when she heard that her youngest son was going to take some time off work. Especially since he and Audra would be able to stay after the party and all through the holidays.

"Jordan, do you have any plans for December tenth? We'd love for you to join us."

Anna's invitation touched Jordan's heart.

Luke wrapped his arm around Jordan's shoulder. "Don't worry, Mother. I plan to do my best to persuade her to come."

"It sounds like a wonderful time, thank you. I'll make sure to put it on my calendar." She smiled as she addressed Luke's mom. "Count me in."

After another couple of hours of chatting, laughing, and discussing plans for the holidays, hugs and well wishes were shared before the five adults finally said their goodbyes.

Monday afternoon, Luke drove out to work on the old house. He was pleased with the progress. So far the renovations were right on schedule. Finishing touches to the dining room were on the agenda today, so he walked back to the laundry room area where he'd stored some of the tools he'd been using. After a few minutes of searching, but still unable to locate what he was looking for, Luke started rummaging deeper through all the cardboard boxes and plastic containers. Noticing there were some other tools missing also, he stood and placed his hands on his hips. Scowling, he went from room to room to see if he'd left them somewhere else. Half an hour later, he gave up. The job couldn't be completed tonight. He double-checked the locks on all the doors and windows before driving home, discouraged and concerned.

The next morning, he drove to the construction site where Carl was supervising a large group of his workers, thinking that maybe he'd brought the missing equipment back for his crew to use and had just forgotten about it.

The two men talked in the backyard, discussing the details of the current project. "Is that why you stopped by? To check on me and the guys?" his foreman asked somewhat defensively.

"No, of course not. I don't have to worry about anything when you're here." Luke then told his friend what had happened and listed all the tools he was missing from the old house.

Carl looked puzzled, but he walked away

from Luke for a few minutes while he inspected the work trucks and then walked
around inside the building they were working
on.

"I didn't see any of the stuff you said was
missing. Could they be in one of the sheds
back at the office?"

"I don't think so," Luke answered. "I
wouldn't have had any reason to take the
tools there." They stood silent for a few
minutes, trying to come up with another solution for the disappearing equipment.

"You sure have been putting in a lot of
hours out there on that renovation," Carl
commented.

"I know, but I want to have it done by
Christmas, and there are still quite a few
things to finish."

The foreman nodded. "I was sure surprised to see you out there Thanksgiving
night though." He chuckled. "I thought you
had big family plans since your brother and
sister-in-law were in town. Does Anna know
that's where you escaped to?"

Luke frowned. "What are you talking
about? I was at my mom's until almost eight
o'clock then drove Jordan home and we hung
out at her house awhile."

Now it was Carl's turn to look confused. "I don't understand. We were driving back from Maggie's folks about ten and when we passed that old place, the lights were on inside the house."

The two men stared at each other for a few seconds. "Somebody must have broken in there and taken my tools." Luke's voice was low and angry, but the mystery appeared to be solved. "I'll make a list of what's missing and contact the sheriff and the insurance company."

A few choice words flowed from his mouth expressing what he thought about the person who had stolen from him. After Luke said goodbye to Carl, he stomped out to his truck.

❀ ❀ ❀

The weekend after Thanksgiving, Luke went over to Jordan's and helped her set up Christmas decorations in the front yard. That Saturday, the residents of Hilldale had awoken to a fresh, new blanket of snow on the ground. Children cheered as they made plans for a morning of snowball fights and sledding before the temperature rose, ruining their fun.

A pair of lighted deer with moving heads were placed next to the small pine tree growing at the edge of her yard. On the ground up by the porch sat colorful red, green, and blue wire boxes that looked like wrapped presents with large bows. They hung several strands of colored lights on the outside of the house as well as hanging several on the bushes and trees. Most of the plastic clips were still attached to the roofline from last year, so that made it easier. The air was crisp, but the sun was out and after a while they didn't even feel the cold. About an hour later, the two stood in the street, admiring what they'd accomplished.

A twinkle flashed in Jordan's eyes. "It looks great, now there is only one thing left to do."

Luke arched his brows. "You have more lights?"

"Nope," she answered over her shoulder with a childish grin as she trotted back to her driveway. "We need to make snow angels."

"Make what?" he asked.

"Come on, it's fun." She plopped herself down in her yard. Flat on her back, she started swishing her arms and legs back and forth in the snow. She looked as if she was doing

jumping jacks lying down. When she was satisfied with her angel, she called to Luke.
"Help me up, please." She raised her arms in
the air. "I don't want to ruin it. Now it's your
turn."

He shook his head. "I'll pass."

Jordan put her hands on her hips. "Oh
come on, it's fun. What's the matter, do you
think you're too studly to play in the snow?"

"I just think it must be more of a girl
thing. My friends and I never did that." Then
he added with a devilish smirk, "But if you
want to see something really awesome, I can
write my name in the snow for you."

She slapped at his arm. "No, that's okay."

Just as they turned to go into the house,
they both burst out laughing. Somehow Odie
had gotten out into the front yard and must've
seen Jordan playing in the snow. The furry
little dog was on his back, wiggling all
around trying to make his version of a snow
angel.

Chapter 18

Luke and Jordan spent as much time together as their busy schedules allowed. She went with him to pick out Christmas presents for his family and volunteered to help wrap them, putting her creativity to good use. The days had flown by and tonight was Anna's Christmas party.

The snow crunched under Luke's truck tires as he drove down Jordan's street and into her driveway. After ringing the doorbell, he heard her yell for him to come in. He'd just removed his coat when she walked into the living room dressed in a red cashmere sweater, knee-length black skirt, and tall, high-heeled black boots that stopped just below her knees. Luke's eyes swept over her, followed by an admiring whistle. "Put a bow around your neck and call me the luckiest man on the planet this Christmas. You look beautiful," he said, his voice low and raspy. Luke closed the gap between them and gave

Jordan a passionate kiss, leaving no doubt that he'd meant what he said.

"Thank you. You look pretty handsome yourself."

He was wearing a deep purple button-up shirt and black dress pants.

They shared a few more kisses, tender and tantalizing. Their breathing became shallow and low throaty noises escaped into the room. When the two of them finally came up for air, Jordan managed to have a moment of clarity. "Luke, we need to stop. We have a party to go to remember?"

"Are you sure you want to leave right now?" he suggested, the huskiness lingering in his voice. "I vote that we stay here and have our own little celebration."

He wiggled his eyebrows while flaunting one of his drop-dead, sexy smiles, complete with dimples. A caressing shiver danced up Jordan's spine like tiny fingers as she gazed into his handsome face. Luke's kisses were intoxicating and addicting. It would be so easy to listen to her heart instead of her head, but Jordan knew if she gave in, they'd never make it to his mother's party. Hormones lost this battle. "Come on, Casanova," she teased him. "We don't want to disappoint Anna."

"Oh all right, but you owe me one." Luke had a surprise up his sleeve, so he knew the night would turn out to be one neither of them would ever forget.

Strings of white lights illuminated the outside of Anna's house, twinkling a warm welcome to the guests as they arrived. A lush evergreen wreath decorated the front door and Jordan inhaled the woodsy, pine fragrance.

"Oh, that smells so good. I remember when I was a kid, my mother would get so irritated when I refused to wash the tree sap off my hands. I'd hold my fingers up to my nose for as long as I could just breathing in that scent. I used to tell my grams that's what Christmas smelled like."

The faraway look on Jordan's face and her hands reaching reverently up to finger the tiny green needles as she told the story of her childhood memory touched Luke. He thought how the small things he'd taken for granted, or never really paid any attention to at all, now took on a whole new perspective through Jordan's eyes.

Inside the house, fragrant candles burned in every room. Embellished garlands draped over the fireplace mantel and above the large arched doorways, creating an inviting atmosphere. The entire house was elegantly dressed for the holidays, but not stuffy. Little touches of whimsy blended well into the overall décor. A group of people milled around the large dining room table where several silver platters of finger foods sat atop a red linen tablecloth. The guests could sample everything from the savory appetizers to the assorted cookies and other tempting desserts. Two crystal punch bowls sat toward each end of the table containing cream-colored eggnog—one "enhanced" with a little alcohol while the other was not.

The guest list had rarely changed over the years, consisting of long-time family friends, neighbors, and members of Anna's charity groups. Jordan recognized several of the people and when Luke introduced her, everyone was pleasant, greeting her with friendly hellos.

Anna chatted with all of her guests as she mingled from room to room, making sure they were having a good time and had plenty to eat. Immersed in her element, she was the perfect hostess. Merriment filled the Kincaid house, adding to the festive mood.

Throughout the evening, Luke and Jordan shared stolen glances. His sinful smiles caused delicious tingles to dance through her. Other times, her cheeks filled with color when he tossed one of his sensuous winks in her direction, usually when she was in a serious conversation with someone important in the community.

Jordan retaliated by sampling the decadent desserts, then slowly licking chocolate or whipped cream from her lips. Once, Luke bumped into eighty-five year old Mrs. Collins, nearly spilling his drink on the top of her head. Since the octogenarian stood only four-foot-six, Anna's son towered over her, making it difficult for him to see her in a crowded room—distracted or not. He quickly apologized to his mother's friend, but age hadn't diminished the feistiness of this senior citizen.

She hoisted her cane and whacked Luke on the shin. "You need to watch where you're going, young man," she scolded before tottering off to refill her cup of eggnog— the spiked batch, of course.

Jordan covered her mouth, doing all she could to stifle a laugh after witnessing the interaction. Luke reached down and rubbed his leg. The look on his face told her he didn't find the encounter near as amusing as she did.

For the safety of the other guests, and themselves, they called a truce by escaping to the
moonlit back porch where they made out for
fifteen minutes, like a couple of sex-starved
teenagers. Wrapped in Luke's strong arms,
Jordan basked in the powerful sensations that
washed over her: excitement, contentment,
happiness. Resting her temple on his cheek,
she closed her eyes and melted against his
chest. Christmas was the perfect time of year
to be in love.

As each guest said good night, they expressed their gratitude to Anna for the spectacular party, wishing her and her family a
Merry Christmas. Eventually, just the five of
them remained. Luke and his mom nodded to
each other, a private communication that
went undetected by the others. "Let's all go
into the family room for coffee then we can
finish decorating the tree," Anna suggested.

Jordan couldn't imagine that any more ornaments could possibly fit on the gorgeous,
twelve-foot Douglas Fir.

Audra kicked off her shoes and eased into
the overstuffed chair next to the fireplace. She
was showing more now than Jordan had
thought she would in the couple of weeks
since she'd seen her last. Philip's wife had

been the belle of the party, looking as stylish as ever while somehow managing to wear her four-inch heels all night. But now she looked tired. The façade had faded. She was just an expectant mother surrounded by the ones she loved.

After the family had a chance to relax and recall the memorable events of the evening, Anna walked across the room to the built-in bookcase. She retrieved a large oak box from the bottom cabinet then set it on the coffee table in front of the couch. The intricate details of the hand-carved design were remarkable.

"It's time for my favorite Kincaid family tradition." When Anna opened the lid, Jordan saw twelve square compartments lined with black velvet, but only five were occupied by stunningly hand-painted, round ornaments. A kind of reverence filled the room as she carefully lifted out a polished silver one. "Merry Christmas, Edward. We all love you and miss you, but we know you're here with us in spirit." Even though the words were spoken softly, they overflowed with sentiment straight from her heart. A shimmering gold one followed, decorated with her name and she loving hung it on a branch near her husband's.

"You're next, Luke," his mom instructed. His was brilliant blue, the color of Anna's eyes, and Luke placed it on the other side of the tree. "Philip, now it's your turn."

Lifting his emerald green ornament from the antique box, he hung it toward the top of the tree.

"Audra, here's yours." Philip cradled a glistening purple one in his hand and gave it to his wife, who proudly hung it next to his. Witnessing the genuine love these people shared for one another, Jordan felt a lump start to form in her throat as she gazed at each of the colorful ornaments displaying the names of Luke's family.

After everyone had taken a moment to quietly admire the tree, Philip reached down and pulled a small white box from underneath the edge of a low hanging branch. "I have another one that needs to be hung." Luke, Jordan, and Anna glanced at each other and back to Philip, curiosity showing on their faces.

"Sweetheart, would you like to do the honors?" Anna's youngest son motioned with his hand.

"I'd love to." Audra turned toward her mother-in-law, pure joy radiating from her face. "I know we'd talked about waiting to find out the sex of our baby, but I just couldn't, so we had an ornament made. We hope you don't mind."

"No, dear, of course not," Anna replied, somewhat stunned at the announcement.

Philip opened the box and pulled out a sparkling pink ornament. "We're having a girl!"

Anna squealed with delight, tears glistening in her eyes as she hugged her son and daughter-in-law.

"Mother, there's one more thing," he continued. "We've picked out a name—Avery. And we want her middle name to be Anna." Philip placed his hand tenderly on Audra's stomach as he gazed into his wife's eyes, unable to contain the overwhelming love in his voice. "Avery Anna Kincaid."

Together, Philip and Audra hung their baby's ornament on the tree next to their own. Tears of love spilled down Anna's cheeks, and once again, she wrapped her arms around her son and his wife. "Thank you. That means the world to me." Her voice quivered.

Luke and Jordan waited until the trio separated before they offered their congratulations to Philip and Audra.

A few minutes later, after giving everyone

THE JOURNEY TO JORDAN 277

enough time to dry their eyes, Luke whispered something into his mother's ear that Jordan couldn't hear. Whatever it was, it produced a soft glow on the older woman's face as she gazed up at him. No doubt it was one of those secret, stolen moments shared between a mother and her child.

Luke peered into the tree with a strange expression on his face then turned to Anna. "Mother, what is that?" He had told Jordan on their way to the party that he'd hidden a present in the tree for his mom and to just play along.

"What are you talking about, son?" Anna squinted, trying to see what he was looking at.

"There, in between those branches next to the gingerbread man ornament." He pointed. "Jordan, can you please help me? You have slender fingers, maybe you can grab it."

She tried to keep the knowledge of the upcoming surprise from showing on her face, not wanting to ruin the moment. She reached in the tree and pulled out a small black velvet box with a gold bow.

She resumed her place next to Luke, looking forward to seeing the excited look on Anna's face when she received the gift. But when Jordan turned back around, she found his twinkling brown eyes staring at her instead, and there in his hand was the box she'd just given to him.

He gazed deep into her eyes. "Jordan, I've known ever since that day I stepped into your flower shop that you were a very special woman. I don't know what I did before you came into my life. No woman has ever made me as happy as you have. Or frustrated me more," he teased. Raised brows above aqua eyes stared back at him. "I've laughed more in these past few months than I have in a long time. I'm sorry, but I lied to you earlier, this isn't a present for my mom. Jordan, I love you with all my heart."

He slowly lowered himself down on one knee and eased open the lid. There resting in the white satin was an exquisite diamond ring. Jordan inhaled sharply, her fingers splayed lightly across her lips. Wide eyes traveled between Luke's face and the sparkling gift in his hand.

"I want to go to sleep with you each night and wake up next to you each morning," he continued, his voice deeply masculine. "I promise to do everything in my power to bring a smile to your face every day. Would you please make me the happiest man in the world and agree to be my wife?"

Jordan couldn't believe this was really happening. She glanced at the other three anxious faces around her and then back down to Luke.

"Jordan, will you marry me?"

"Oh, Luke! Yes! Yes, I'll marry you!" Her heart pounded so hard, she was sure everyone else could hear every beat. Taking her left hand in his, he slipped the ring on her trembling finger. Her knees grew weak. She felt lightheaded and pleaded with the bones in her legs to support her so that she wouldn't faint.

As soon as Luke stood up, Jordan threw herself into his arms. "I love you so much."

Their lips met, and for a brief moment, they were the only two people on earth. Everything else just faded away.

Cheers of congratulations from the excited bystanders filled the room, penetrating the couple's blissful haze. Anna and Audra wrapped their arms around Jordan as tears flowed freely.

Philip slapped Luke on the back. "It's about time big brother." Then he added with a sly grin, "Good choice."

When all the commotion died down and a

box of tissues had been passed around one more time, Anna got everyone's attention. "There have been so many wonderful surprises tonight, but I have one more." Bending down, she lifted another box from underneath the tree. "Jordan, I knew about the engagement ring all along," she said, smiling lovingly up at her oldest son. "So this is for you. I'm very pleased that you are going to part of our family, and I couldn't think of a better way to welcome you." Anna removed the cover and nestled in gold tissue paper, was a glistening red ornament with Jordan's name on it.

Stunned by the thoughtful and unexpected gesture, Jordan felt as if her heart was going to burst from all the love and happiness she'd experienced tonight. Her eyes traveled from Luke to the gift. "It's beautiful!" Her voice quivered as she looked into the face of her future mother-in-law. "Thank you, Anna." She gently lifted the ornament from the box and hung it next to Luke's. Tears flowed again as heartfelt emotions—strong, almost tangible— filled the room.

"This calls for a celebration!" Philip said, stepping out of the room. He soon returned with four flutes of champagne, along with a glass of sparkling cider for Audra. Raising their drinks, they toasted the two new additions to the Kincaid family.

Luke cleared his throat and looked over at Jordan. "I do have one condition on my proposal."

"Oh?" Her curiosity was peaked, wondering what it could be.

"I want to marry you right away, so I was thinking we could tie the knot right after Christmas, on the twenty-eighth. How 'bout it?"

Jordan stared at him in disbelief, "Of this year? Two and half weeks from now?"

"Yes, ma'am. I want to start the New Year as husband and wife. Besides, I don't want to wait any longer than absolutely necessary to go on our honeymoon," he added with a wickedly sexy wink, knowing it would make her blush.

The women snickered and Philip burst out laughing as a rosy pink colored Jordan's cheeks.

"I'm not sure I can pull a wedding together that fast."

"The majority of my family is right here in this room, and didn't you say Andy was going to be visiting you over the holidays anyway? We'll keep it small. I've already talked to Pastor Green, and my friend, Tom, from the event center. They have us penciled in. And you can handle the flowers."

A sassy smirk formed on Jordan's lips. "You were pretty confident that I'd say yes, weren't you?"

Luke wiggled his eyebrows. "I can be pretty irresistible when I put my mind to it."

"In your dreams maybe," Philip scoffed sarcastically, shaking his head.

Audra scowled at her husband, "Be nice." She gave him a quick smack on his leg for emphasis.

"There's my dress and the cake and the food and—"

"We'll help!" the other women chimed in unison.

"I know some great shops in the city to get wedding dresses," Anna volunteered.

Audra nodded. "I'll look them up on line and make a list."

"I'll take care of the caterer," Anna added.

Jordan looked around at her new family. She beamed as happy tears pooled in her eyes. "It looks like I'm outnumbered, so if you think we can actually pull this off...then let's do it."

Cheers and shouts of excitement filled the room. The clinking sound of five crystal flutes rang out as they toasted again.

While the women huddled together chattering about this and that to do with the wedding, Luke pulled Philip off to the side. "It would mean a lot to me if you'd agree to be my best man.

The look of genuine happiness in Philip's eyes revealed his answer. "I'd consider it an honor."

Luke detected a slight catch in his brother's voice. They exchanged a quick one-armed hug and slapped each other on the back the way men do when expressing their feelings while at the same time trying to maintain their macho image.

"I hope you're not upset about the timing of my proposal," Luke mentioned a moment later.

"No." Philip shot his brother a puzzled look. "Why would you say that?"

"I just don't want you to think I was trying to steal the limelight and overshadow your wonderful announcement. I had no idea that you had such great news about the baby to share tonight, too," Luke explained with sincerity.

With a dismissive wave of his hand, Philip looked at his older brother. "Don't worry about it. Audra and I are really happy for you and Jordan. Besides, mom's over the moon." The brothers glanced at their amazing mother, the devoted matriarch of the Kincaid family. "She has so much love to give, and I bet she'd tell you that our announcements will be the two best presents she'll receive this Christmas." The two men nodded in agreement before joining the rest of their expanding family.

Jordan, Audra, and Anna agreed to get together the following Saturday so they could spend the day shopping for the wedding.

A little while later, five very happy, but tired, people took turns hugging each other goodbye. Anna squeezed Jordan tight and kissed her cheek before whispering in her ear, "I'm so thrilled to have Millie's granddaughter as a part of my family."

Jordan closed her eyes, trying to fight back the tears as her arms tightened around her future mother-in-law.

"Thank you," she managed to breathe. "For everything."

The two women shared a knowing look before Luke helped Jordan with her coat and whisked his bride-to-be out into the chilly night air.

Humming quietly, she snuggled up next to him in the truck while Christmas music flowed from the stereo speakers and drifted around them.

"Did you have a good time at the party?" Luke asked, half teasing.

"Yeah, but I had more fun after the party." Holding out her left hand, Jordan admired her ring again before laying her head back on his shoulder.

Luke placed a kiss the top of her head, "I'm glad."

"I can't believe you proposed!"

"Are you disappointed that I did it in front of my family instead of just the two of us some place romantic?"

"Absolutely not. I wouldn't have wanted it any other way. They're great and I'm so happy that they'll soon be my family, too."

Warmth spread through Luke's body. "Yeah, I'm a lucky guy." Jordan's answer just made him love her more.

After he walked her inside the house, she offered him some coffee. "No, thanks. But I will have some of this." Pulling her to him, he slid his hand behind her neck, burying his fingers in her silky brown hair. "I love you," he breathed just before pressing his lips down on hers.

Jordan moaned softly as she molded her body to his. As the minutes ticked by, their kissing became more passionate and intense.

Lifting his head, Luke gazed deep into the aqua eyes that had stirred him from their first meeting. "Maybe we should take a stroll down the hall to your bedroom and rehearse for the wedding night. You know what they say, practice makes perfect. Whadya say, beautiful?" His dark brows arched mischievously, hoping to convince her to give in.

Tingling shivers raced through Jordan as she envisioned Luke making love to her. "I have no doubt that it would be wonderful." She offered him a bright smile. "And as much as I want to be with you, I want our wedding night to be romantic and special. Besides, you only have to be patient for about two more weeks. I'm sure you'll survive."

Powerful churnings of desire and love raged inside of him, but her happiness was more important. Staring deep into her eyes, he tenderly brushed the back of his knuckles against her cheek. "All right," he whispered. "You're definitely worth waiting for." He'd have a lifetime to caress the feminine body standing in front of him, the one he'd fantasized about all these long months. Leaning close, he kissed her again, passionately and thoroughly. She melted in his arms, sharing several more kisses before he left.

After Jordan went to bed, she replayed the events at Anna's house. She really did love Luke, and now she had no doubt that he loved her, too. She kept fiddling with her engagement ring, twirling it around her finger, just to make sure she wasn't dreaming. When she finally drifted off to sleep, she dreamt of Luke and their wonderful life together.

Chapter 19

Early the next morning, Jordan called Andy. It had been too late last night and she couldn't wait any longer to share the good news with him. Just as she was about to hang up, a sleepy voice answered, "Hello."

"Andy? Are you still in bed?"

"M.J.? Yeah, I've been fighting a cold the last couple of days."

"I have something very important to tell you," Jordan gushed. "So wake up."

"Okay, okay, I'm up. What's so urgent it couldn't wait until later?"

She took a deep breath. "Luke asked me to marry him last night!"

"Oh, that. Yeah, I already knew about it," he responded, still a little groggy.

She frowned. "What do you mean you *already* knew? How could you? It just happened."

He had to finish a yawn before he could

answer. "Luke called me a few days ago and asked for my blessing. He's a stand-up guy. I guess since you don't have a father to ask, he came to me, and I was more than happy to say 'yes.'"

Jordan processed what he had just said. "Thank you, Andy. You may be my kid brother, but I'm glad he thought enough of me to ask you first. Well then, that will make what I have to say next a little easier. It would mean a lot to me if you'd walk me down the aisle at my wedding."

"I'd love to, Sis. I was hoping you'd ask." A moment of silence passed, "Can I ask you something, M.J?" The quiet, serious tone in her brother's voice told her whatever he was getting ready to say was important to him.

"Of course, Andy. What is it?"

"Do you wish dad were here to give you away?"

A whirlwind of images raced through Jordan, and she took a minute before she answered. "No, I don't. He made his choice not to be a part of our lives all those years ago. I've forgiven him for what he did to our family. I finally realized that holding on to the hate was only hurting me—and he wasn't worth it."

After another short pause, Andy spoke. "Okay, well I was just wondering, cuz I know that's a big deal to brides."

"You were my first and only choice because it was partly your fault we're together," Jordan teased, wanting to lighten the mood.

"My fault?" He searched his brain to make sense of what his sister was saying. The night of the auction suddenly popped into his head. "Oh, you mean because I signed your name on his donation at that charity thing?"

"Well, I suppose that played a role, too. What I meant was, Luke found my old journal somewhere. You know, I never asked him where he got it." Strange how the thought hadn't crossed her mind before now. She'd have to remember to do that. "But I do remember having to hide it from you because you were such a terror when you were young. If I wouldn't have had to stick it in the wall, I may have remembered to take it with me when we moved."

"Hey, you had some great stuff in there," Andy reminded her.

She shook her head, remembering her little brother and his tormenting her when she was a teenager.

"Oh, did Luke also tell you he wants to

get married in two weeks? Crazy, huh?"

"Yeah, he mentioned that. He probably doesn't want to give you time to change your mind." He'd never get too old to razz his big sister.

"Very funny." Jordan laughed into the phone. The two chatted a little while longer about their work.

"I have one more question for you. Does he make you happy, Sis? I mean really happy?"

"Yes, Andy, he does. I love Luke very much, and I know we're going to have a wonderful life together."

"Then I'm happy for you." He paused again. "Do you need me to do anything before I come out?"

"Not that I can think of right now, but I'll let you know."

"Okay, and congrats, Sis. You deserve to finally be happy."

Her brother's voice was kind and sincere.

"Thanks, Andy. I can't wait to see you. I love you."

"Love you, too, M.J."

They were relaxing one evening, curled up on Jordan's couch talking about the wedding. She noticed that Luke seemed distracted and unusually quiet. "Is everything okay?"

"Of course. Why?"

His halfhearted answer did little to convince her. "What's going on? If something is bothering you, I'd like you to tell me. After all, I'm going to be your wife in a few days."

He shifted his position so they were facing each other. "I want to ask you a question."

A serious expression crossed his face and his tone concerned her. Jordan's heart started to race as painful scenarios rushed through her mind. *Has he changed his mind? Does he want to call off the wedding?*

Trying to control the anxiety in her voice, she stared into his eyes, hoping to find the comfort his words were not communicating. "All right," she said, bracing herself for the worst.

Luke hesitated. "I...I was just wondering if you've ever heard from your father or have ever tried to find him."

In one sense, she was relieved that her initial fears were wrong. But, she didn't want to discuss this with him—open old wounds. Not now when she was so happy and her life was turning out just like she'd always hoped it would. A part of her knew he had the right to know. Somewhere deep inside, Jordan sensed if she told him, the secret and the shame would no longer be able to haunt her. Taking a deep breath, she answered, "No, I never have."

Silence hung heavy between them. Luke knew this was difficult for her and felt sorry he'd asked. "I'm—"

"Don't." She stopped him. "I need to tell you. I need you to hear the whole story."

He leaned back against the couch and nodded.

"You obviously know some of the story from my journal. What you don't know is how the money my father stole devastated the lives of the people in this town. People lost their homes, their businesses, their farms, and even..." Jordan felt her throat start to close. Tears welled up in her eyes.

"Oh, sweetheart, I didn't mean to upset you." He tried to pull her into his arms, wanting to comfort her, but she resisted and placed her palms on his chest.

"I want to get this all out in the open then put it to rest and never talk about it again," she insisted.

Once more, he nodded and let her continue.

"A man died because of what my father did." Jordan saw the shock on Luke's face at her announcement. "Arthur Murphy was an older gentleman who'd worked at the bank for thirty years. I'd like to believe that my father had no idea Mr. Murphy was there that night. Arthur came out of his office when he heard the commotion and stumbled upon my father filling duffle bags with money from the safe."

Luke frowned. "Your dad shot him?"

"No, but Arthur confronted him and said he was going to call the police. He was on his way back to his office when my father grabbed him and tied him up while he finished gathering the cash. When the bank president arrived the next morning, he found Mr. Murphy and called an ambulance. He was rushed to the hospital where doctors discovered he had a broken rib and several bruises. The police were able to speak with him a few hours later about what had happened the night before. He died later that evening of a heart attack caused by the traumatic situation at the bank and the struggle with my father.

"Mother couldn't comprehend how her

husband could do something so horrible. Mr. Murphy's adult children would call her and yell horrible things at her constantly. One day, Arthur's wife came to our house. I thought Mother was going to faint, but she invited her in and they talked for two hours behind closed doors. Mother never would tell me the details of their conversation. The only thing she ever said about it was that there would be no more phone calls—and there weren't.

"Now do you understand why I was so angry about you finding my journal at your house and about the conversation I heard?" Jordan's eyes searched Luke's face for a sign that pouring her heart out to him had been the right decision.

Cupping her cheek, he wiped away a tear with his thumb. "Yes, Jordan, I do."

"I was terrified that if you found out about my past, you'd want nothing to do with me and—that you could never love me, especially if you knew the truth about my father." Her voice trembled and tears rolled down her face.

He lifted her chin so he could look into her sad eyes. He desperately needed her to believe what he was about to tell her. "I never would have judged you by what your father did, Jordan. He made some very bad choices. I'm so very sorry that he put you and your family through all that pain. I can see how difficult it was for you to share what he did, and I'm so glad you could. But it's out in the open now, and your past can never come between us again."

This time when he reached for her, she allowed him to pull her into the safety of his arms. Things were going to be all right. She'd faced one of her worst fears and was emotionally and mentally exhausted, yet relieved, as she let the tension in her body drift away, wrapped in his strong embrace, surrounded by his healing love.

During the next week, Luke and Jordan had scheduled several appointments. They met with the event planner about the details for the reception then went to the newspaper to place their wedding announcement. There was no time for formal invitations, so they contacted people by phone or in person, inviting them to the reception. Only family and a short list of close friends received a special hand-delivered note. Wednesday, they sampled several cake flavors and combinations, finally deciding to alternate between vanilla and chocolate in the first three layers, with the top tier being a marble cake. Jordan described, in detail, its appearance to the woman at the bakery.

The following Sunday afternoon, Jordan, Anna, and Audra drove into Portland. Christmas decorations lined the streets, white lights and tinseled stars hung from the light posts along with giant red bows. Businesses had their windows frosted and painted with Santas and snowmen. The chill in the air added to the atmosphere and magic of the season.

They eventually found one of the shops in the Pearl District that Audra seen online. After Jordan had tried on five or six gowns, the sales woman brought out one more. Jordan stood on the round platform in front of the three-way mirror and stared at her reflection. "Am I being silly to want a white dress and all the bells and whistles? I'm almost thirty years old. I don't exactly fit the typical stereotype for wearing a white dress. Don't you think people will find it a little...I don't know...strange? "

Anna took Jordan's hand in hers. "This is

your wedding. You should do whatever you want. Besides, when my son sees you walking down the aisle toward him in that dress, it's going to take his breath away."

Jordan turned back to face the mirrors, running her fingers over the white fabric, "All right ladies, in that case, this is the one. *This* is my wedding dress," she announced with tears in her eyes. It was a beautiful gown and it fit her perfectly. It didn't need any alterations, just a little pressing, which was good, because there wasn't time for the standard fittings, nips, and tucks.

While Jordan changed clothes, Luke's mom talked to the manager about a quick fix for the dress she'd found to wear. Taking a seat next to Audra on one of the plush sofas scattered throughout the store, Jordan turned slightly toward her. "I know we haven't known each other very long, but we are going to be family, so I was wondering if you'd agree to be my matron of honor."

"That is so sweet of you to ask, but if I get up in front of the church looking like this in a bright red dress, people will think I'm Mrs. Clause." She chuckled softly as she rubbed her stomach.

Picturing the scene, Jordan snickered too.

"You'd look gorgeous no matter what. Please do me a favor and just think about it, okay?"

Audra nodded, hugging her future sister-in-law.

After Anna joined them, they left the bridal store and found a restaurant nearby where they could grab a bite of lunch. Conversation flowed easily among the three women as they decided on what stores they still needed to visit. They were finishing dessert when Anna excused herself, and Audra leaned close to Jordan. "I've thought about the question you asked me earlier."

Jordan's eyes locked on the other woman's face in hopeful anticipation. "And?"

"I'd consider it a privilege to accept, as long as you don't mind standing next to a plump matron of honor." Audra sweet southern voice made it sound like she was accepting an academy award.

"That won't bother me at all." Jordan's eyes brimmed with tears. "Thank you so much."

Anna was just returning from the ladies room. "What's all the whispering about?"

Jordan told her future mother-in-law the good news and all three women used their linen napkins to dab the corners of their eyes.

Shopping continued throughout the afternoon for other wedding odds and ends, some festive holiday decorations, and extra red ribbon for the flowers. Jordan didn't want the normal plastic bride and groom cake topper, so when she found a crystal one with two intertwined hearts, she knew that it was the perfect choice. She also bought Luke's wedding ring. It was a simple gold band, no diamonds, no frills.

Back in Hilldale, Luke and Philip went to pick out their tuxes. Jordan had given them both strict instructions not to choose any weird colors and no ruffled shirts, like in that Jim Carrey movie. The men strutted around the store, showing off each outfit, much to the delight of the female customers. The women enjoyed the antics of the handsome brothers, acting as if they were posing for a photographer. Luke and Philip made their decision, with the help of the manager, Cindy, who had received a visit from Jordan a few days earlier to discuss acceptable options for the two men. She'd made Cindy promise not to tell Luke that his fiancé had been there to curb any "creativity" he might think appropriate for their wedding.

Their next task on the list was to confirm

the arrangements for the reception and pay the deposit. A couple of other quick "honey-dos," and then Pastor Green was their final stop. Once everything at the church was confirmed, Luke and Philip went to the steakhouse down the street. Over dinner, Philip reminisced about his wedding to Audra.

Luke told his brother he had one more place he needed to go before driving him back to their mother's house. "I need to pick up Jordan's wedding ring and the surprise present I ordered for her."

"Present? Are you trying to spoil her already? You need to save that kind of kissing up for after you're married, like when you do something stupid and have to get back in her good graces."

Luke laughed. "Thanks for the marital advice little brother, but I think I'll handle things on my own."

"Rookie," Philip huffed, shaking his head as he followed Luke into the jewelry store.

Right before Jordan closed up her shop the next Tuesday, she heard the bell above the front door chime.

When she rounded the corner, there was a woman standing next to the silk flower arrangements.

"May I help you?" When her customer turned around, Jordan thought she looked vaguely familiar, but couldn't quite place her.

"Are you Rebecca Price's daughter?"

Jordan swallowed hard as an icy wave of panic rushed through her. "Yes," she replied.

"I'm Cathy. Arthur Murphy was my father."

Jordan's heart pounded in her chest, and she gripped the counter for support. The nightmare she'd had so many times was finally a reality—and it was staring her in the face. She knew she should say something. "I—I'm so sorry—"

Holding up her hand, Cathy stopped her. "My mother asked me to come and talk to you. She wanted me to apologize for how horribly our family treated yours years ago. We realized after a while that we took our anger out on the wrong people. You all weren't to blame for what your father did," Cathy said, while her trembling fingers fidgeted with the buckle on her purse.

Jordan was shocked. "Thank you. But I know my mother was very upset about what happened. She wanted to tell your family, but under the circumstances..."

Cathy glanced down at her shoes before she continued. "We also need you to know how ashamed we are that our actions caused her to think that she had no choice but to pack up her children and leave town. My mom wants to make it clear that my family has no hard feelings against you."

"I appreciate that," Jordan said. "I'm just not sure the rest of the town will be so forgiving once they find out who I am."

"Actually, our family is one of the few that are still here. Some have moved away, some of the older folks have died, and as you can see, Hilldale has grown a lot since you left. My mother, along with the other families that still remember what happened, have discussed the situation. You don't have anything to worry about. Nobody will harass you or tell anyone about your background."

Jordan could feel tears of joy and relief sting her eyes. "Please tell your mom how grateful I am to her, to all of you."

The two women stared at each other for a few seconds as the years of fear, anger, and heartache melted away.

"I guess I should be going now," Cathy

said, offering a cautious smile. "You have a lovely shop here, and I'll be back in a few weeks." She saw the look of confusion on Jordan's face. "You see, my mother is dying. She made me promise to come and buy the flowers for her funeral from you." A tear rolled down Cathy's cheek, and she swiped at it with her fingertips.

Jordan's heart went out to the woman in front of her. She walked over and placed her hand on Cathy's arm. "Whatever you need, just let me know. I'd be honored to make the flower arrangements for your mother. And don't worry about the cost, please accept it as my gift to her." Jordan saw the appreciation in Cathy's eyes when she nodded in response.

"Thank you," she whispered, her voice ragged with emotion. "I'll let Mom know."

After Arthur Murphy's daughter left, Jordan locked the front door. She went into her office and sat down. She felt drained. Finally her past was no longer a threat to her future.

Chapter 20

A shadowy figure dressed in black emerged from behind the house, the gray hair above his ears poking out from underneath a worn ball cap. It was one o'clock in the morning, but he still stopped at the corner of the building and peered into the darkness, making sure he was the only one around.

After tossing two canvas bags in the back seat, he slid behind the wheel of the rusted old Buick and turned the key in the ignition. The car inched down the long gravel road, which was lit only by the moon. The man's eyes strained to see where he was going. When the car pulled out onto the main road, he flicked the headlights on. An evil chuckle escaped his lips as he glanced over his shoulder at the bags resting on the vinyl seat behind him. *It won't be long now and I'll live the rest of my life in paradise.*

He missed the beaches where he'd spent

the last several years. He wanted to hurry back to the young, sun-worshiping, bikini-clad females who were always ready to keep a man company—for a price. Money made him attractive to exotic and beautiful women half his age. It was the reason he'd needed to make one last trip back to Hilldale. He'd had to retrieve the last of the bank money he'd buried behind the old house. Now he could forget that this place had ever existed.

The faces of his two children suddenly appeared in his mind, producing a slight twinge of regret in the deep recesses of his chest, where he'd stuffed their memories so long ago. It had been almost ten years since he'd seen them. He obviously wouldn't be nominated for any awards when it came to his track record as a father. Even if he looked for them, he doubted they'd speak to him. Shaking the thought from his head, he realized it didn't matter anyway. His life was far away from here, where the only two things he needed were a willing female and some shots of tequila.

A few miles later he relaxed, unaware that a dark blue sedan had joined him on the otherwise deserted road, careful to stay several car lengths behind.

The men tailing him in the sedan were in no hurry to catch up to the Buick. They had finally found him. Now they would wait until just the right time to make their presence known and spoil all the plans that Stewart Price had made.

Early the next morning, Jordan had just stepped in the back door to the flower shop when her cell phone rang. "Hello."

"Ms. Shaw, this is Agent Fuller. I wanted to let you let you know that we apprehended your father last night just outside of town."

Jordan gasped. Her hand flew to her chest. "Really?" she whispered then started to cry. "So, it's over—it's finally over?"

"Yes, ma'am," the agent replied.

"Thank you for calling. I really appreciate it."

Luke drove out to the old house Friday morning to make sure everything was ready for tomorrow night. Pulling into the yard, he noticed fresh tire tracks in the dusting of snow that had fallen yesterday afternoon.

There were footprints, too. He followed them around the side of the building. When he walked into the backyard, he saw that someone had dug a large hole over by the woodpile. Upon further inspection, he discovered a metal barrel buried in the ground. There had only been about a foot of dirt covering the top of it. That's how whoever had been here was able to retrieve what was inside. The ground was too frozen to have dug very far beneath the surface. A string of questions popped into Luke's mind. *Who did this? What could they have hidden in the barrel? Why did they wait until now to come for it?*

After staring at the opening for a few more seconds, he reached for his cell phone and called the sheriff's office. While he was waiting for Mike, he took a look inside the house, hoping nothing had been disturbed. A thorough search reassured him that everything was fine.

Mike Wilson showed up about twenty minutes later. He looked around the backyard, made some notes, in addition to taking pictures of the tire tracks, shoe prints, and the area around the exposed barrel. The sheriff was just as baffled as Luke about the mysterious hole. The officer wrote up a report and said he'd keep Luke informed. But since nothing else besides Luke's previously stolen tools seemed to be missing, Mike didn't hold out much hope the mystery would be solved.

Jordan closed her shop early Friday in order to work on the flowers for the wedding. *Her* wedding. It was still hard for her to believe that she was really getting married, and to someone as wonderful as Luke Kincaid. It didn't take her long to finish the boutonnières for Luke, Philip, and Andy.

Luke's contained two red roses mixed with holly. He would be wearing a black tux, white shirt, and red vest so she knew this would be the perfect combination. For the other two men, she wrapped standard greenery around a single white rose. They would be wearing the same basic tux as Luke, but their vests were black instead of red.

Next, was Anna's corsage. Jordan knew she was wearing an emerald green dress so she selected one red and one white rose, adding ribbons and greenery for the final touches. Audra's bouquet consisted of white roses with accents of holly, bringing out the touches of red to match her dress, with red ribbons wrapped around the stems of the flowers.

She was just about to start on her bouquet when she heard someone banging on the front door. The Closed sign was up, so she decided to ignore whomever it was, hoping they'd eventually go away. But the knocking continued, and now it was accompanied by a muffled, yet frantic sounding voice. It was no doubt a forgetful husband who'd suddenly realized today was his wedding anniversary. She finally decided to go and inform the man that he'd just have to buy his flowers somewhere else. When Jordan rounded the corner, the man saw her and banged even more fervently on the door.

"Ms. Shaw! Ms. Shaw, I need to speak to you on an urgent matter!" he panted, a frenzied look in his eyes.

"Sorry, but I'm closed," she said, gesturing toward the sign, plainly visible in the store window.

"No, wait, please! You don't understand. I need to talk to you immediately! It's of the utmost importance!" The man looked a little familiar to Jordan, but then she'd seen so many people lately with planning the wedding and all, she couldn't remember how she knew him.

He appeared to be on the verge of a

stroke, so she felt the least she could was find out what he wanted.

"Calm down, sir. Forgetting your anniversary is no reason to make yourself sick. I'm sure your wife will understand."

The man squinted at Jordan. "Anniversary? What are you talking about?"

"Isn't that why you're banging on my door?"

He frowned. "No, I'm not married."

"Well, whatever the reason is, you'll have to come back another time because I'm closed for two weeks." She turned to walk away, but what the flustered male voice said next made goose bumps crawl across her skin.

"I think there's been a terrible misunderstanding, Ms. Shaw. I'm Stanley Pickett from the law offices of Dwyer and Haywood. I have a letter here from your grandmother, Millie Harper."

Jordan froze, her head pivoted sharply in the direction of the shop's front door. She stared at the man on the other side of the glass, positive she must have heard him wrong. "What did you say?"

"I'm from the attorney's office that handled your grandmother's estate, and I found a letter that had been misplaced all these years. I assumed it was important for you to have it." Mr. Pickett removed an envelope from his jacket pocket and held it up for her to see. "Can I please come in?"

Jordan was in shock as she unlocked the front door. "I don't understand," she mumbled.

Stanley was barely five seven and probably weighed a hundred and twenty pounds soaking wet. He definitely fit the stereotypical description of a nerd: wire rimmed glasses perched on a narrow nose and he shook like a nervous Chihuahua. Once inside, he removed his black fedora then began patting his forehead and face with the handkerchief he'd pulled out of his back pocket. It was cold outside, but he was behaving as if it was the middle of July. "Thank you, Ms. Shaw. I know my visit is unexpected, but I wanted to give you this letter. I found it on the floor behind an old filing cabinet in the storage room. Our research discovered it was supposed to have been delivered to you after Millie's death. As a representative of Dwyer and Haywood, I'd like to offer our sincerest apologies for any trouble or inconvenience this situation may have caused you."

"Do you always deliver lost letters in person?"

"No, but this is an unusual circumstance. You see your grandmother had mailed this to you, but for some reason it was returned. Shortly afterwards, she passed away. The nurses then packed her belongings into a box and gave it to my firm. We found this among her things when we were settling her estate. Unfortunately, we misplaced it," Stanley said sheepishly.

Jordan looked at the postmark on the letter in her hand. She realized it was sent right after she moved from one apartment to another. *I wonder why the post office didn't forward it to me.* "That still doesn't explain why your firm didn't just mail it to me once you knew I was back in town."

"It's a rather delicate matter."

Jordan arched her eyebrows. "Oh? Well maybe you should explain it to me."

The nervous little man mopped his forehead again. "If you insist. Your grandmother and Mr. Haywood were, um..." He stopped and cleared his throat. "They..."

She rolled her eyes. "For goodness sakes, just tell me. They what?"

He drew in a long breath. "They became

very close friends after Mr. Haywood's wife passed away." Stanley prayed that Jordan wouldn't ask him for more information. But he was immediately disappointed.

"What do you mean, '*very close friends*'?"

"Mr. Haywood cared a great deal about your grandmother. Before she went into the nursing home, they used to go out to dinner or to the movies. They enjoyed spending time together."

Jordan's eyes widened. "They were...dating?"

"Yes, I presume some people would call it that. So when we found the letter, Mr. Haywood wanted to be sure the situation was handled in person instead of just putting the letter in the mail to you." He saw her face soften, and he was relieved that she seemed to be satisfied with his explanation.

She had to smile as thoughts warmed her heart. *So Grams had a boyfriend. Wait until Andy hears about this.* She looked at the man standing in front of her. "Thank you, Mr. Pickett for bringing this to me. Please tell Mr. Haywood how much I appreciate the fact he saw to it that I received my grandmother's letter."

"I will, Ms. Shaw," he said, before placing

his hat back on his head. He turned and scurried out the door, grateful to have that assignment over with.

Jordan was still confused and shocked by the quick arrival and departure of her peculiar visitor, not to mention the fact that she was holding a letter from her grandmother. She re-locked the front door and wandered back to her office. Lifting the small, yellowed pages from the dirty envelope, she focused on her grandmother's handwriting. Tears made it hard to read the words, but after dabbing her eyes with a tissue, she tried again.

My precious, M.J.

I'm sure by now you're very upset with me about the stipulation I put in my will. Trust me, it's for the best, you'll see. You need to break free from the chains that bind you to your past and the only way to do that is to face them head on back here in Hilldale. I can hear you arguing with me that you're not strong enough or some hogwash like that, but you are. The M.J. I love is smart and determined. You can take on the world if you just

have faith in yourself. You have noth-
ing to be ashamed of, it wasn't your
fault. It was that no-good putz of a fa-
ther that caused all the trouble. Don't
let what he did destroy the rest of your
life.

I hope your flower shop will do
great. You always seemed so excited
about working at the one where you
went to college. I could hear it in your
voice. The creative ideas you have are
wonderful! Who knows, maybe some-
day you can even come up with a flow-
er and name it after me. Wouldn't that
be a hoot!

By the way, I met a very sweet
woman who volunteers a couple time a
week here at the assisted living center.
We became instant friends. We talked
about books and gardening and cook-
ing. And yes, we talked about our fami-
lies. We showed each other pictures,
and we exchanged funny stories of
when our kids were little. Her husband
became ill and she had to quit. I miss
her, but she still stops by when she

can. She has a very handsome son a couple of years older than you. When you move back to town you should go introduce yourself. Her name is Anna Kincaid.

I love you very much my darling granddaughter and someday you'll understand.

Grams

First, she cried because she missed her grandmother so much. She had been a wise and special woman.

Jordan hated the fact that she'd never see her great-grandchildren. But in spite of the tears, she couldn't help but laugh at the words her grandmother wrote at the end of her letter, and somehow wondered if Grams *did* have anything to do with her meeting Anna's handsome son.

Just then, Luke walked in the back door. Jordan had said she'd leave it open for him if he wanted to stop by. When he saw that she'd been crying he took her in his arms. "What's wrong? Why are you upset?"

She relayed the events of her surprise visitor and then handed him her grandmother's letter.

After reading the first part, he asked, "Stipulation?"

"In order for me to get my inheritance, I had to move back here. She also asked that I use the money to open my own business."

"So *that's* why you came back home."

"Yeah, Grams always said and did whatever she wanted. She didn't beat around the bush when she had an opinion about something that was important to her," she said with a chuckle while wiping away the rest of her tears.

Luke's eyes opened wide when he read the last part. "She was really something else. I wish I could've met her. I know I would've loved her."

"She would've loved you, too. I can't wait to tell your mom about the letter." Jordan knew Anna would find the words of her old friend amusing.

The two talked about their wedding. He decided not to tell her about the trouble out at the house, especially since it would ruin his surprise. Jordan showed him the flowers she'd done so far, and he raved about how beautiful they were. He asked about her bouquet but she refused to tell him. "You'll just have to wait until tomorrow," she teased.

He took her in his arms, desire sparking inside him. "I can't wait to marry you, my love." Pressing his lips to hers, he felt her respond. The softness of her mouth fueled his need for her. Several minutes later, breathless and panting, they finally separated.

Tomorrow night she would be his wife and the thought of finally making love with him, sent a shiver racing down her spine. "I think you better go now. I have a lot of flowers to assemble and you're too much of a distraction."

He reached for her again. "I'll leave after a few more kisses."

The roguish and smoldering look on his handsome face was almost more than she could resist. "Mr. Kincaid, don't make me throw you in the walk-in cooler," Jordan threatened with a smirk. A deep, throaty rumble came from deep in his chest. She beamed. "Now, go. I'll see you tomorrow."

"You can count on it." He tossed her a wink as he strolled out the back door. "I can't wait to finish what we started this afternoon."

Chapter 21

Jordan and Audra arrived at the church three hours before the wedding. The decorations were festive and colorful. Darcy had helped her with the finishing touches last night, but now, with the sun shining in the windows, it looked even more breathtaking than she'd remembered. Hanging on the end of each wooden pew down the center aisle were swags made of Douglas Fir, small pinecones, and holly, tied with red bows.

The whole scene brought tears to Jordan's eyes, especially when she spotted the surprise Luke had mentioned.

There, in the front of the church, stood a pair of ten-foot tall Pinion Pines and their scent filled the sanctuary. Their branches were thick and decorated with tiny, white Christmas lights, red bows, and red and white glass ornaments.

Surrounding the base of each one were pots of white Poinsettias wrapped in cranberry-colored cellophane that sparkled, reflecting the lights from above.

Originally, when they were making their plans, Jordan had been disappointed because they weren't going to be able to have real trees. Most of the ones that had been used for Christmas around town were now dried out, posing too great a fire hazard. She stared in shock at the live trees. *Where did they come from?*

While Audra went to find the room where she'd be helping her soon-to-be sister-in-law get ready, Jordan made her way down the aisle to get a better look.

Pastor Green had heard someone come in and joined her at the front of the church. "Good morning, Jordan. You've done an amazing job, young lady. It's going to be a beautiful wedding."

"Thank you. But how? I—" she stammered pointing at the stage, before glancing over at him.

The minister handed her a small envelope before going back to his office to prepare for the ceremony. "I think this will explain everything." She sat down on the front row and pulled out a handwritten note. It was from Luke.

Jordan,

I knew you had your heart set on real trees for our special day, so instead of cutting down more, I bought these from the nursery. We'll plant them at our new house after we're married and then we'll always have a piece of today near us.

I wanted you to have the smell of Christmas for our wedding. I hope they make you smile.
All my love,

Luke

Her eyes drifted from the tender words to the thoughtful expression of his love. Wiping the dampness from her cheeks, she joined Audra. Tears of joy threatened to fall again with every step of her transformation from the ponytail-wearing, flower-shop owner to the radiant bride that would soon become Luke's wife.

Her dress was simple, but elegant. The white, form-fitting, silk gown was adorned with a few small crystal and pearl accents on the bodice. Adding a touch of playfulness to the outfit, she'd decided it would be fun to wear red high heels under her dress.

Just as Audra was finishing Jordan's make-up, there was a knock on the door. "Go away, Luke," Audra warned. "You can wait a few more minutes."

"It's Andy," a muffled voice said from the hallway. "Can I come in?" He eased the door open and peeked inside, not waiting for a response. After taking a couple of steps into the room, he studied the woman in front of him as if looking at a stranger. "Wow, Sis, you look amazing." His tone was hushed, almost reverent.

"Thank you," she whispered, tears filling her eyes.

"Don't cry," Audra cautioned. "Or we'll have to start your make-up all over again."

"I know, but I'm just so happy. You understand what it's like. How it feels to be marrying the man you love." Jordan saw a wistful, far away expression come across Audra's face.

"Yes, I remember," Audra said, gently touching Jordan's arm. "Well, it's a good thing I used water-proof mascara." The women chuckled while Andy just stood there, not quite sure what to do or say. "I'll leave you and your brother alone for a little bit." Audra smiled. "But then I'll be back to add the finishing touches—and fix any damage."

"Are you sure I look okay?" Jordan asked, her nerves requiring a little reassurance from a male perspective. She turned toward the full-length mirror, her trembling hands gliding over the white fabric around her stomach and hips.

"You're beautiful, M.J.," Andy replied looking over her shoulder at their reflection. "But I think you're missing something." A grin that Jordan remembered from their childhood crossed his lips. "I have something for you that I think will go pretty well with what you're wearing."

She looked at her brother, wondering what he could be talking about. "Oh, really? And what would that be?"

"This." A gold jewelry box sat in the palm of his hand.

"What it is?"

"Open it and find out," he prodded sarcastically.

"Oh, Andy, you shouldn't have."

"I didn't." He paused seeing the creases appear on her forehead. "It's from Luke."

She held her breath for a moment then took a seat at the mirrored vanity. Inside the box, she found a large pair of sparkling diamond earrings and a small note.

I wanted you to have these for your "something new." I can't wait to be your husband.
Love, Luke

With trembling fingers, Jordan managed to put them on. Love welled up in her again as she looked in the mirror.

"Aren't they beautiful?" The happiness in her voice was undeniable.

"Not even close to as beautiful as you look wearing them." Andy's voice was soft and loving.

She picked up a small paper fan and waved it in front of her face in an effort to stop the tears from falling. "That's very sweet, but you're not supposed to make me cry, remember?"

"You better keep that thing handy," her brother warned.

"Why?" she asked, her gaze still focused on the ceiling.

"Because," he said, walking up behind

her, "I'm in charge of the 'something old.'"
He slipped a diamond and ruby heart pendant
around her neck.

When Jordan felt cold metal against her
skin, she looked into the mirror again and her
heart stopped. "Is this...Where did you..."

"Yup, it's Gram's."

Fresh tears pooled in her eyes as she
fought down the lump forming in her throat.
After brushing her fingertips over the heir-
loom, she glanced at Andy. "But how—"

"Before mom died, she sent it to me with
instructions to give it you on your wedding
day. It's been in a safety-deposit box all this
time."

Jordan's mom and grandmother had both
worn this necklace on their wedding day. "I
wish Grams and Mother could be here today."

Andy laid a gentle hand on his sister's
shoulder and nodded toward the necklace.
"They are, Sis."

A knowing smile and an unspoken understanding passed between them as flashes of
her childhood rushed into Jordan's thoughts.

"Okay, enough of this mushy stuff, M.J.,"
he announced, not wanting to let on that his
own memories were obscuring his vision.

"I'll go find Audra so she can finish helping you get ready."

In another room on the opposite side of the church, Luke was losing his battle with the black bow tie for his tux. Swearing under his breath, he released an irritated sigh.

"What's the matter big brother?" Philip chuckled. "Can't get dressed by yourself?"

The sharp glare Luke shot him relayed the message that he was in no mood for his brother's wisecracks, but it also held a plea for assistance. Philip helped Luke with his tie but couldn't resist one more jab. "I didn't think I'd see the day when you'd find a woman willing to put up with you," he added with a teasing slap to Luke's back.

"Gee, thanks."

"But seriously, Jordan's a great girl. You're a very lucky man."

"I know, and I'm going to do whatever I can to make sure she never regrets her decision."

Just then, Pastor Green knocked on the door. The three men shook hands and went over the details of the ceremony again. The minister then turned his attention toward Luke. "Are you ready to get married, young man?"

"Yes, sir. I most definitely am."

"Good answer, Luke." The pastor smiled. "All right then, let's go wait for your bride."

When Audra returned, the two women spent the next twenty minutes oohing and ahhing over the earrings and necklace. Then they took care of the last minute details while Andy waited outside in the hall. Finally, they heard organ music coming from the sanctuary—their cue it was time to go.

Audra kissed Jordan on the cheek before turning to leave. "I'll see you at the front of the church." Andy held out his right arm and Jordan placed her hand through the crook of his elbow, wrapping her fingers around the sleeve of his tux. As they approached the foyer, a tender smile eased onto his face. "I love you, Sis."

"I love you too, little brother. It means more to me than you'll ever know that you're here to walk me down the aisle."

"I wouldn't have missed it for the world. Are you ready to become Mrs. Luke Kincaid?"

Happy tears glistened in Jordan's eyes. "With all my heart."

The organ began playing "Here Comes the Bride," and the guests stood in unison. Jordan took a deep breath and nodded to her brother just before they entered the sanctuary. She immediately searched for Luke at the front. He looked even more handsome than she'd even imagined, standing there in his tux. As their eyes locked, her nervousness disappeared. Her heart overflowed with love for the man waiting to become her husband.

Luke inhaled sharply when he saw how gorgeous Jordan looked, fully aware of how blessed he was to be able to spend the rest of his life with this special woman. He swallowed hard. The sight of her made it hard for him to breathe.

It seemed to take forever for her to join him, almost as if she were walking in slow motion. Andy placed his sister's hand in Luke's then lightly kissed her cheek.

"You are so beautiful," Luke whispered next to Jordan ear. "Nice shoes," he added with a wink. He watched the color tint her cheeks above her playful smile.

Pastor Green motioned for the guests to sit, before focusing his attention on the bride and groom.

The ceremony was intimate and full of personal touches. Staring deeply into each other's eyes, Luke and Jordan recited the vows they'd written for one another. The love in the room was tangible to all in attendance.

It was time to exchange rings and Pastor Green turned to the groom. Luke twisted around and looked at Philip, holding out his hand. The best man checked his pants pockets, shrugged and shook his head at his older brother. Luke began patting the jacket of his tux and then stuffed his hands in the pants pockets.

A low murmur rose from the guests. Jordan couldn't believe he'd forgotten their wedding rings. She leaned forward slightly. "Luke, what's going on?" she whispered impatiently through gritted teeth.

Luke gazed at his bride. "I, ah, I can't seem to find—"

She caught a roguish sparkle dancing in his dark brown eyes as if he'd suddenly remembered where they were.

"That's right, I have a surprise for you. I got permission to have someone very important in your life bring in the rings." He nodded his head toward the back of the church, and the double doors opened wide. Down the aisle trotted Odie, wearing a black bow tie and carrying a small velvet bag. The little dog held his head high, as if sensing that his job was important. Snickers, gasps, and a couple of people added an, "Oh, how cute!" and "Isn't that sweet!"

Jordan's hand flew to her mouth, seeing her furry friend included as a part of the wedding. With Andy following close behind, Odie pranced up to the very front of the church and sat down right by the bride and groom.

Tears overflowed down Jordan's cheeks. "Thank you." She beamed at Pastor Green and her sneaky almost-husband.

Reaching down, Luke tousled the fur on Odie's head then took the bag from his mouth. Andy and the dog took their seats on the front row.

"Here you go." Luke placed the ring in the minister's palm, and they finished saying their vows.

"I now pronounce you husband and wife," Pastor Green announced. "Luke, you may kiss your bride."

"My pleasure," Luke declared in a clear, vibrant voice, his deep dimples on display for all to see.

The guests cheered and clapped. Even Odie barked his approval resulting in a burst of laughter that filled the sanctuary.

After walking back down the aisle, the newlyweds received hugs and best wishes from their guests in the foyer. Carl was congratulating Luke when Darcy scurried up to Jordan. "That was so awesome, boss. You look totally smokin' hot." Jordan thanked her and introduced her to Luke.

"Hey, Uncle Carl, I'm surprised to see you here." The young woman pointed at the newly married couple. "How do you know them?"

"Luke's my boss," he responded. "What about you?"

"No way! Are you serious?" Darcy starred at the gray-haired man, "Jordan is *my* boss." The four of them shared a chuckle at the coincidence.

Jordan studied Carl. "You wouldn't happen to be the uncle that helped with the van's flat tire that time, are you?"

"Yes, ma'am, that was me."

She reached over and placed her hand on his arm. "Thank you so much for all you did."

Her eyes shone with the sincerity of her words as she told Carl the story of what happened and how that was the day she'd mistaken Audra for Luke's wife.

Once all the guests had left for the reception, the newlyweds posed for pictures. Andy took Odie home and told his sister he'd see her at the party. Jordan went to find Anna and wrapped her in a warm hug. "I just wanted to thank you for raising such a wonderful son. He's a good man." She stepped back and looked down at the floor, heat coloring her cheeks. "I wasn't the easiest person to get to know and I didn't make it easy on him."

Luke's mom took Jordan's hand, but didn't respond, somehow knowing her new daughter-in-law had more to say.

"I also want to thank you for welcoming me into your family like you have. I don't have anyone left except my brother..."

"My dear, you are a treasured addition to our family. I feel like the most blessed woman on earth. I raised two wonderful sons and now I have two extraordinary daughters. My family finally feels complete."

The lump in Jordan's throat was getting larger from all the love she'd experienced these last few hours. "I was just wondering if it would be all right if I called you "Mom," especially after today. I've come to love the whole family and it just seems natural to think of you that way."

"I'd like that, Jordan." Anna patted the

corners of her eyes with a tissue before hugging the newest member of her family again. "I'd like that very much."

Chapter 22

Hidden among a thick stand of trees at the edge of the park, pale green eyes peered through the branches at the old stone church across the street. The air was heavy with the unmistakable and fragrant scent of pine trees, mingled together with the earthy smell of wood smoke from fireplaces ablaze in the homes nearby. He'd been standing there, waiting, for almost forty-five minutes to catch a glimpse of the woman he'd come to see, glancing around every now and then to make sure he remained undetected. Over the years, his worn jacket had lost some of its ability to block out the elements. Shivering as a burst of icy wind whipped around his face and down the neck of his shirt, he leaned forward slightly, huddling against the cold. His ears tingled painfully in the winter air and his nose had started to run, so he swiped at his face with his sleeve.

After taking one more long drag on his

cigarette, he ground it into the snow with the toe of his boot. He knew they were bad for him and at one time he'd thought about quitting. But six months ago, when doctors told him the cancer that was eating up his insides would kill him long before the smoking did, he figured there was no reason to stop now.

That was why he needed to see her one more time.

He blew on his hands and rubbed them together. Folding his arms across his chest, he tucked his numb fingers under his armpits. The lone figure shifted and swayed back and forth, lifting one foot out of the snow and then the other, trying to keep his circulation moving. Even though the afternoon sun shone brightly, he lingered in the cold shadows. The rays transformed the random sections of undisturbed snow into patches that sparkled as if topped with sugar crystals. He wished he'd brought his flask of whiskey with him to calm his nerves and thaw him out a little. But too much self-medication caused him to become careless, and he couldn't afford to make an error in judgment—especially not today.

Brightly-colored Scrub Jays squawked and squabbled high in the trees. As they hopped from limb to limb, the loose snow that lay on the tips of the branches cascaded down around him. When a breeze filtered through the pines, it swirled the white specks against his skin, stinging like tiny needles.

His sister had emailed the wedding announcement from the newspaper, but he'd forgotten to write down the exact time. Now he wished he had. At least he'd remembered how cold it got here in December and he was glad he'd worn an extra pair of socks. If he hadn't, his toes would be frozen inside the scuffed and scarred leather boots. Shielded from the sunlight by the towering trees, four inches of snow still covered the ground where he stood. Maybe he shouldn't have come, but his counselor was always yammering some crap about needing closure in order to be able to move on with his life. If only he'd had the courage to go to her and try to explain the circumstances of why he'd left. But the woman he'd come to see had already been through so much misery in her life, he'd felt it would be selfish of him to re-open old wounds now just to clear his conscience. He'd left town like a coward, running from the people that cared about him the most. Telling her he was sorry seemed so insignificant in the grand scheme of things.

It would be like trying to use a single glass of water to extinguish a raging forest fire.

Useless.

Sounds from across the street, carried by the icy wind, reached him. He glanced up as a group of people dressed in their tuxes and gowns filed out of the church. A lump formed in his throat when he saw the bride. She was so beautiful in her flowing white wedding gown, her face beaming with love as she looked up at her new husband. The sight of her tugged at his heart. *She finally looks happy*, he thought. The man in the park could only stare at the precious part of his past he'd left behind all those years ago. Memories flashed in and out of his mind like a fast-paced slide show, each frame lasting only seconds before the next one took its place. This guy, whose name he couldn't remember, better treat her right and love her like she deserved to be loved. Lord knows *he'd* made a mess of things.

Suddenly, M.J. looked around and scanned the edges of the park. He stood as still as a marble statue, holding his breath, but his pulse raced. He couldn't let her see him. Although he didn't believe she would recognize him unless she was standing right in front of him. Even then, he had his doubts. His cheeks were sunken, his face drawn and thin, and his eyes, which had once held a zest for life, were now vacant. He was a mere shell of the man he used to be—that man had died a long time ago. It seemed like another lifetime. After she turned back to her friends, the man hiding in the shadows exhaled a sigh of relief. The puffs of steam from his breath floated around his head before dissipating in the branches of the trees.

A gust of cold wind instantly triggered another sharp twinge in his shoulder. The wound from the past reminded him of things and experiences he'd fought so hard to forget all these years. He automatically reached up and rubbed the throbbing joint hoping to get some relief. As he attempted to rotate it, an immediate, stabbing pain shot down his arm and he grimaced.

"Have a good life, M.J.," he whispered. "I never stopped loving you." Not being able to endure the ache in his shoulder any longer, he realized it was time to leave. He'd accomplished what he'd come to do—to say goodbye one last time.

To help block out some of the December chill, the man pulled up his collar before shoving his hands deep into the pockets of his faded, green military jacket. Then Brad turned and disappeared unnoticed across the park, leaving his hometown and M.J. behind once again—this time forever.

"It's time to get to the reception every-one," Luke announced. He helped Jordan and his mother with their coats, then the five of them stood outside on the church steps chat-ting a few more minutes before driving to the event center.

Luke noticed Jordan's eyes searching the area across from the church with a concerned expression on her face. "What's wrong?"

"I'm...ah, not really sure. It just feels like someone is watching us."

Luke slipped his arm around her waist. "Well, I don't see anyone, but if there is somebody out there staring it's because they're mesmerized by how gorgeous my wife is."

She chuckled. "I think you are going to catch on to this husband thing just fine."

They arrived at the reception to the hoots and hollers of their family and friends. White lights twinkled from the ceiling, casting a warm glow over the entire room, making it cozy and romantic. Bowls of red, green, and silver ornaments accented with sprigs of pine and holly sat on each table.

After dinner, they mingled with their guests and danced to several of their favorite songs.

Luke pulled Jordan into a darkened corner of the room and gazed deep into the aqua eyes of his new bride. "Have I told you in the last few minutes how much I love you, Mrs. Kincaid?"

"Yes, but I'll never get tired of hearing you tell me, Mr. Kincaid." Her heart was so full of love she thought it would burst right out of her chest. "I'm so happy that you're my husband. Thank you."

"For what?"

"For making this the happiest day of my life and not giving up on us."

He gently kissed her lips. "Anything for you, my love."

During one of the slower songs, he whispered, his voice raspy, "How much longer do we have to stay here?" He wiggled his eyebrows at her. "I want you all to myself so we can get the honeymoon started. As beautiful as you look in that wedding dress. I can't wait to get you out of it."

She blushed and poked him in the ribs. "Soon," she answered, rubbing her body against his.

The movement produced a growl from deep in his throat. "Sweetheart, you better stop that, especially when you know I can't do anything about it here with all these people watching."

"Anticipation is a powerful aphrodisiac," she teased.

All right. Well, two can play that game. He started nuzzling the spot just below her ear. He felt her body shudder and she stumbled. "Now we're even," he added with a smirk of satisfaction.

When it was time to cut the cake, a warning look from her reminded him of her earlier threat of severe bodily injury if he smashed cake on her face.

Once the last person was thanked and hugged goodbye, Jordan and Luke strolled hand in hand out to her SUV. Seeing her reflection in the side mirror, she caught a glimpse of something sparkling on her earlobes. "Oh, I almost forgot. Thank you for my earrings. I love them."

She placed a sweet kiss on his cheek.

"I'm glad." He winked at her. "*You* make them look good." He reached in the backseat and handed her a wrapped box. "I have another present for you."

She tore off the gold and green Christmas paper and lifted the top. Inside she found a black leather book. It was a new journal embossed with their names and today's date.

Her eyes met his, and he just smiled. "Open the cover and read the inscription."

> *To My Wife, Jordan,*
> *Your old journal brought us together, but was a part of your past. THIS journal represents a new beginning of our lives together. I love you very much.*
> *Your husband, Luke*

Deep emotions swamped Jordan's heart as she held the precious gift to her heart, overwhelmed by this thoughtful gesture of his love. Words wouldn't come, but she could tell Luke understood the meaning behind each tear that rolled down her face.

"I still have one more surprise for you."

"Really? What—is it?" she sputtered

while trying to pat her cheeks dry. She didn't know how much more she could handle today.

"You'll see," he said with a mischievous gleam in his eyes. "But you need to wear this blindfold."

Jordan's damp eyes squinted at him. "You're kidding right?"

"No, I'm not." He secured the strip of cloth over her eyes and drove the SUV toward the edge of town.

"Where are we going, Luke?"

"Just a little bit longer, sweetheart."

Finally, he turned down the snow-covered driveway. After shifting the vehicle into park, he said, "I didn't make the reservations at the hotel like you asked, so I hope this will be okay for our wedding night."

"You didn't?" Her voice held some concern. "Then where are we?"

Opening the passenger door, Luke lifted his bride gently to the ground, guiding her up the steps. "I love you with all my heart, Jordan. I hope you like your biggest surprise." He paused. "But I might need a little insurance." Leaning down, he wrapped his arms around his new wife, kissing her passionately.

"You must have really messed up, so just

remove this thing so I can see how badly," she muttered after catching her breath.

He playfully reminded her, "What was that you said earlier about anticipation?"

"Luke, be serious, besides, it's cold out here."

"Okay, but you have to keep your eyes closed." He reached up and untied the strip of black cloth. "Now on the count of three, you can open your eyes." In order to draw out the suspense, he took his time counting. "One—two—"

Jordan reached her hand out to swat at him, but missed. "Oh, for Heaven's sakes, will you quit goofing around and hurry up?"

His teasing continued. "Now I have to start all over. One—two—two and a half—"

"Luke!"

"Okay." He chuckled. "Three."

When she first opened her eyes, she wasn't sure where she was, but suddenly the memories came rushing in. Confused, she glanced at Luke. "This is—"

"Yes, Jordan. It's your grandmother's house.

Her hand few to her mouth as a small whimper escaped her lips. "Oh, Luke." She threw her arms around her husband's neck.

Not sure if she was happy or upset, he looked at her, trying to read her eyes, but the answer wasn't there. "Jordan, are you all right?"

"I can't believe you did this!" She reached out lightly touching the etched glass on the front door with her trembling fingertips.

"Are you ready to go inside?" His voice was tender with love.

Jordan just nodded, wiping away a tear.

He put the key in the lock then swept her up in his arms.

She squealed. "What are you doing?"

"I'm carrying my beautiful bride across the threshold. It's tradition, you know," he stated in a matter of fact tone before kissing the tip of her nose. Their laughter filled the air.

When he carried her through the doorway of the old house, he remembered the first day they met and how she'd felt in his arms then. "I know it's not exactly like when you lived here, but..."

After he flicked on the lights, he lowered her feet onto the wooden floor while his left arm remained around her waist. She gazed around the room, studying all the changes that he'd made.

"Maybe not, but it's amazing! I can't believe you did this!"

"So you approve of what you've seen so far?"

"Oh, yes. I think it's wonderful."

He smiled. "I'm glad."

As her eyes continued to wander, her vision suddenly froze on an old, treasured memory—one she'd believed had long ago been lost or destroyed. There on top of the fireplace mantel sat the worn, but precious, nativity scene belonging to her grandmother.

"Is that..." Jordan gasped, turning toward Luke. "It can't be..." she whispered, her voice filled with a mixture of uncertainty and hope.

"I found it in the attic and I knew it had to be a part of our first Christmas—and every other Christmas together in this house," he explained with a gentle smile.

He saw shock and confusion in her eyes. "I bought this house and remodeled it. This is *our* house now, my love. We'll start some traditions of our own and keep some from when you lived here. I have a special piece of wood in the pantry for marking the height of the kids on their birthdays." He paused, his voice softer. "It's right next to the one you and Andy had."

Tears streamed down her face as she remembered her past here. They continued to fall as she pictured a future with her husband and children together in this house.

Looking deep into his wife's dazzling blue-green eyes, Luke lovingly whispered the words he'd been wanting to say for several weeks.

"Welcome home, Jordan."

About the Author

Debbie Lee was born and raised in South Dakota, but currently lives in Arizona with her 9 year old tabby cat named Lucy. She raised 2 daughters, Nicole and Katie, and she is extremely proud of the wonderful women they have become. She has worked for the State of Arizona as an Administrative Assistant for the last 22 years. Lee started writing in 2009 and enjoys reading contemporary romances mixed with a little humor. She's thankful to God for all the blessings in her life and for this new adventure as a writer. Lee is a huge animal lover, and especially enjoys spending time with her four-legged Chihuahua "grandchildren," Bruiser and Dottie.